SLEEP LIKE THE DEAD

A CHARLETON HOUSE MYSTERY

KATE P ADAMS

Paperback ISBN 978-1-7335619-3-8

Cover design by Dar Albert

ALSO BY KATE P ADAMS

THE CHARLETON HOUSE MYSTERIES

Death by Dark Roast

A Killer Wedding

Sleep Like the Dead

A Deadly Ride

Mulled Wine and Murder

A Tragic Act

A Capital Crime

Tales from Charleton House

THE JOYCE AND GINGER MYSTERIES

Murder En Suite

For Joshua,
welcome to a family of bookworms.

'*W*ell you wouldn't catch me sleeping in here, not for love nor money. I can't believe people are paying to spend a night tossing and turning on these cold wooden floors. It's like a military camp. You're not even giving them beds.'

Joyce tutted before striding across the room and peering closely at a portrait of a young child from the 17th century. 'Dear God, I pity that child's parents, having to stare at that creepy mug all day.'

She had a point, it wasn't the most flattering portrait of the toddler, dressed strangely from head to toe in a smock and bonnet. Its protruding eyes and lips made it look as if someone was attempting to pump air into the child to see if it would pop. It was the kind of portrait that belonged in the attic.

'Just think of how much money they'll spend in the shop,' I offered. Joyce Brocklehurst managed all the gift shops at Charleton House, so I hoped that idea would cheer her up.

'They better had, we're opening early tomorrow morning and I have overtime costs to cover.' She strode off down the room, checking out more paintings as she went. I watched, fascinated by the pile of blonde hair on her head, her trademark bouffant as steady as a Roman column, not a wobble in sight. She turned slowly and steadily on her four-inch wedge heels, and surveyed the scene.

'Barmy, every one of them – £150 to spend the night sleeping on the floor of a creaky, draughty 500-year-old building.' She made her way back along the length of the room and rolled her eyes as she walked past me. 'Rather you than me, Sophie,' was her parting shot as she disappeared through the door.

I was left alone in the Long Gallery, the silence unnerving. Against the maroon velvet flocked wallpaper, portraits of the Fitzwilliam-Scott family members stared out at me, each one seemingly assessing my respectability and suitability to be gracing the hallowed halls of their palatial home. I half expected one of them to come alive and shout for a guard to escort me out.

But I very much belonged here at Charleton House, the home of one of England's most significant aristocratic families. The current Duke and Duchess resided on the floor above; the rest of the house was open to the public, and this evening sixty of them would experience a night in the splendid baroque building. Admittedly, as Joyce had observed, they were having to sleep on the wooden floor of the rather chilly gallery, but on the other hand, they would get to do what usually only family members and their personal guests got to experience: sleep amongst the art and antiques of one of the country's most outstanding historic houses.

These sleepovers occurred very infrequently and the tickets were much sought after. The evening's guests would be taken on tours and told tales that hadn't previously been shared with the public, hearing secrets and becoming acquainted with scandals that had occurred in the very rooms they were exploring. They would be entertained by characters from centuries past, and dine on food that my chef had researched and ensured fitted in with the theme for the evening.

Fortunately, I wasn't responsible for the whole shindig; that daunting role lay in the hands of Yeshim Scrimshaw, the events manager. I only really had to worry about the food, and as the Head of Catering, I'd worked with my chef to make sure we would offer a fun and interesting menu. One of the three cafés I managed would become a dining room for the night, and we would ensure our guests had constant access to hot drinks and, more importantly, a supply of biscuits. This wasn't the first of these events we'd run, and if there was one thing we had learnt, it was that biscuits could fix every problem, calm frayed nerves and ease the frustration of a sleepless night.

'So, tonight is your lucky night.'

I hadn't heard Mark Boxer enter the room so I jumped as he drawled his words into my ear, sounding like a medallion-wearing, chest-hair-revealing lothario. I turned to face my friend, who had a smirk on his face, and looked at him blankly, hoping he would explain. I'd always considered it a great honour to work in such a magnificent building, but tonight was going to be a lot of hard work, and he made it sound like I'd won the lottery.

'I bet you never thought you'd get to spend the night with me. We can create special moments throughout the evening, and then in the morning...'

'You can go home to your husband,' I interrupted.

'I was going to say that I'd do my best to be gentle while leaving you with a broken heart and unbeatable memories, but have it your way.'

I laughed as Mark feigned hurt and dramatically straightened his tie. Not that it needed straightening. Just like the rest of him, it was impeccable. The knot was perfectly tied, his waistcoat had the bottom button undone, as had been the convention from at least the Victorian period up to the present day; his handlebar moustache was waxed and curled, his suit spotless, and his shoes reflected the light from the chandeliers.

'Are you really staying the whole night?' I asked.

3

'No, not really. I figured I'd deliver my tour, stay for the rest of the entertainment, and then head home before the clock strikes twelve and I turn into a pumpkin. You?'

I shook my head. As loyal as I was to Charleton House, I drew the line at sleeping on a wooden floor. I checked my watch and swore – I had work to do.

Mark was fiddling with a watch he'd pulled out of a small pocket in his waistcoat. The gold chain matched his tie clip.

'Nice – new?'

He nodded. 'Early birthday present from Bill, he thought I might like to have it for this evening.' Mark gently wiped the glass.

'It's your birthday this week?' I asked in mock surprise. 'I had no idea.'

Mark raised an eyebrow as he put his present away. 'Really? Then I guess that carrot cake I saw cooling on a rack this morning must be for someone else.'

Damn, he'd seen it. I was hoping to keep it a surprise. I had yet to finish it, but in theory I had plenty of time before the get-together that Bill, Mark's husband, was hosting for him on Monday, his actual birthday.

'Come on, old man.' I took his arm and turned him to face the door. 'I have work to be getting on with, and if you've nothing better to do than creep up on unsuspecting women, you can give me a hand.'

Mark allowed himself to be led out. We were about to take our first steps down an ornately carved wooden staircase when a scream made us jump. It was followed by the shattering of glass and a tirade of shouting. I grabbed Mark, who steadied himself on the banister, and by some miracle neither of us fell. I had known this would be an eventful night full of drama, but hopefully of the entertaining kind.

I let go of Mark's arm and ran down two steps at a time. It seemed that the curtain was already up and the show had begun.

. . .

Yeshim Scrimshaw was standing in the middle of a sparkling sea of broken glass. Anger was etched on her face and she was glaring at a young blond-haired man in a small, partly concealed doorway. He was trying to hold back laughter.

Yeshim has an almost superhuman ability to remain calm, and we were getting a world-class display of her skills. For all his sniggering and nonchalance, the young man still hadn't moved. I guessed he was just a little afraid of the outcome if he did.

With a coldness that matched the sharp edges of the glass that lay around her, Yeshim spoke slowly, never once taking her eyes off the object of her measured wrath. After she'd finished telling him what she would do with him if he ever tried to surprise her like that again, she turned her attention to me.

'Sophie, I do apologise. Thanks to this buffoon's attempt at humour, I'll need you to fetch another thirty champagne flutes. I was transferring them through to the Gilded Hall so we could set up for the welcome drinks. That plan has, however, been thwarted.'

I stepped off the bottom stair and reached for the empty tray that hung by her side.

'No problem, Yeshim, I'm on it. I'll call housekeeping and ask them to come and clear this up. Mark, why don't you take our young friend here and put him out of harm's way?'

I looked over my shoulder before leaving and saw Mark rest a hand on the young man's shoulder and steer him out of another door. Yeshim gave her head a little shake and a smile returned, if a little mechanically. Clapping her hands, she sent everyone on their way. The first mishap of the evening had been dealt with.

'He's called Douglas Popplewell. He worked in the ticket office for a couple of years, and then started as a tour guide about three months ago, although he's been guiding in other buildings in Derbyshire as a volunteer for a few years. He could be worse. A bit overenthusiastic and more of a showman than I like, but that will calm down with time.'

Mark was filling me in on the young man who had jumped out at Yeshim. Apparently he'd thought it would be funny, but he hadn't spotted the tray of glasses in her hands.

'He's trying to play it cool, but you can tell it's an act. He thinks he can charm everyone, but it doesn't work on Yeshim – she can see straight through him.'

We were lining up sixty flutes, ready to be filled with champagne and handed to the evening's guests as they arrived. Yeshim was in a corner on her hands and knees, fiddling with a plug socket. The budget for this event wouldn't stretch to live music, so small modern speakers were concealed at the bottom of the grand marble staircase.

I nearly dropped a glass and added to the evening's tally of breakages when a burst of ABBA at full volume echoed around the room.

'Sorry,' shouted Yeshim as she turned it down. 'Wrong playlist.'

The more calming notes of Mendelssohn drifted out as we polished the glassware and Mark continued to tell me about his newest tour-guiding colleague.

'He can keep a crowd's attention, it's quite impressive really. But he needs to put more time in behind the scenes. He doesn't always get his facts right. The public generally don't notice if he's a year or two out on his timelines, or gets the Duke's great-great-uncle's cousin's name wrong, but it's unprofessional and drives me barmy.'

Mark continued to talk as my mind wandered. I was always slightly in awe of the imposing marble staircase that dominated the room and the gilded balcony that ran around all four sides, giving the space its name. We were being watched over by gods and goddesses who inhabited the fresco on the high ceiling.

'Are we ready?' Yeshim had composed herself and her calm, cheery voice was back. 'Where's the Duke and Duchess? They need to be here to greet everyone. What about the servers? They should have the champagne on trays.'

'Coming, I'm here, I'm here.' Betsy Kemp, or rather Henrietta Fitzwilliam-Scott, the 8th Duchess of Ravensbury, came flying down the stairs two at a time. The crinoline that puffed her dress out around and behind her made it drag on the carpet and was in danger of sending her tumbling as she ran.

'Where's the Duke? He's late,' Yeshim called as the Duchess jumped the last few steps and landed in front of her.

'He's struggling with his necktie, but he's right behind me.' Betsy was out of breath. The calm stately demeanour of a 19th century Duchess was nowhere to be seen; instead, she was red-faced and panting. Her hands planted firmly on her hips, eyes closed, she turned her head up to the ceiling. 'I really need to get fitter.'

'Or set off on time,' Mark muttered to me. 'Betsy's always doing this, the others are really good at adlibbing her late arrival for every scene she's in.'

'Time,' I shouted. 'Time, Betsy, you've still got your watch on.'

Betsy glanced down at her wrist.

'Bugger. Thanks, er...'

'Sophie.'

'Sophie, right, here.' She ripped the watch off her wrist and tossed it across the room at me. Fortunately, my schoolgirl rounders skills didn't let me down and I caught it, shoving it in my pocket.

Yeshim started organising things again.

'Where's the Duke?' she repeated. 'The guests are arriving. I want everyone in place when they walk in.'

I'd heard the chatter over the radios and knew that some of our overnight guests had already arrived. They were being taken first to the Long Gallery to drop off their belongings and claim a spot on the floor with their sleeping bags. Once they were ready they would be escorted, many of them in costume, here to the drinks reception, the first event of their packed schedule. I looked out of a window onto a courtyard and could spot a few of them being escorted by the warders on duty that night.

The warders' regular work was during the day when they would be in the house, talking to the public, sharing stories with them and making sure they didn't climb on furniture or touch the delicate and extremely valuable objects on display. At night, they helped out on events, and this evening a small team was staying over to support Yeshim and her staff.

The sound of someone running along the gilded balcony caused our heads to swivel and we watched as Harvey Graves, dressed as James Fitzwilliam-Scott, the 8th Duke of Ravensbury, came thundering around the corner towards the top of the stairs.

'DON'T RUN!' bellowed Mark. 'The Conservation Department will do their nut if they see you pounding along the balcony.'

'Sorry, sorry,' Harvey replied breathlessly. He too jumped the last few steps and landed next to his 'wife'. Between deep breaths, he leaned over to her.

'That bloody woman is here, I've just seen her arrive. She's all petticoats and cleavage.'

'Conrad was wondering if she'd turn up,' replied Betsy. 'I hope Lycia controls herself and we don't add fireworks to the evening's itinerary.'

They grinned at each other, and after straightening themselves out, they looked just like the portrait of the couple painted in 1865 – the year in which this evening's events were set – that hung in the Long Gallery, a reference that some of the guests might spot, if they hadn't consumed too much alcohol.

'Who are they talking about?' I asked Mark. He shook his head and let out a long sigh.

'If it's who I think it is, then we're going to have our hands full. Philippa Clough, blogger, Dickens addict, and subject of previous scandals.'

2

Mark and I stood back and watched as the guests started to arrive. Some had clearly popped to their local costume shop and wore cheap 'historic' dress that didn't really fit any era. Modern shoes peeked out from under their hems, watches were on their wrists, and there was a century-leaping display of jewellery. They entered laughing, their excitability ramping up as they took in their surroundings and helped themselves to a glass of champagne.

Others were clearly obsessives who had spent days and probably weeks bent over sewing machines, surrounded by dress patterns and determined to get every detail right. The room was quickly filling with top hats and bonnets, and many of the women wore gloves that reached their elbows. Heavy silk mingled with velvet in a variety of hues, from sombre greens and blues to bright reds and pinks, with a few stripes thrown in for good measure. A couple of women had even poured themselves into corsets; it was going to be interesting to see how they fared in those, especially after the hearty meal that I knew Gregg Danforth, my chef, was cooking up for them. There were more women than men, whose costume contributions ranged from a reluctantly donned top hat and cane, to full evening attire with fitted waistcoat and tailcoat. It looked like a cross between a film set and a steampunk party.

This was a million miles away from my previous jobs, running cafés and restaurants in London. There I usually only dealt with city types in dull suits, talking about the stock market. This couldn't have been more different and it was wonderful. I looked down at my navy blue suit. I'd brightened it up with a vivid orange silk shirt, but I still felt dowdy compared to the peacock-like display before me.

'He doesn't look too happy.' I nodded in the direction of a middle-aged man who wore an oversized tailcoat over a pair of jeans.

'He'll be fine once Dr Alcohol has loosened him up. Which might be sooner than you think,' Mark commented. We watched him grab a second glass whilst simultaneously emptying his first.

Some of those who had made less effort looked a little crest-fallen as they took in the works of art that others wore and, in some cases, had probably cost hundreds of pounds. They in turn looked snootily down their noses, no doubt viewing themselves as the true aficionados who in a parallel world would have lived somewhere as beautiful as Charleton House. The 8th Duke and Duchess circulated in all their finery, making their way to every guest as they arrived, complimenting them on their outfit, no matter how much effort they had made, or not. They asked them about their journey, if their horses were tired or if their coach driver had found a room in the local inn.

Betsy and Harvey were experienced members of the live interpretation team. They weren't just actors, they were passionate educators who carried out research and inhabited a role, taking pride in their ability to remain in character no matter what bizarre questions the public tried to flummox them with. I watched the Duke discuss the unusual fabric and design of some-one's trainers as though he'd never laid eyes on them before in his life, wondering if they had travelled from the Orient or Americas and commenting that he was sure they would never catch on in England.

'There she is.' Mark was discreetly pointing to a large-bosomed woman in a straw-yellow silk dress. Despite having been one of the first to arrive at the house, Philippa Clough had engineered a grand entrance as the last to arrive at the reception. Her dress projected out, keeping people at arm's length, flounces of material making it appear large enough to house a small family. The low-cut neckline was trimmed with lace, drawing my eye down to her cleavage, which was indeed quite startling – you'd have to be blind, or dead, not to notice.

'She doesn't have to open her mouth and she's the loudest in the room,' Mark observed. 'Ah, there's her little coterie.' He nodded towards a couple that Philippa had spotted and was dramatically sweeping towards across the room in their direction. Giving them both exaggerated kisses and twirling in front of them, she laughed as she clutched her corset. 'Thomas and Annie Hattersley. Annie always comes to events with Philippa, but is a mouse in comparison. Hard to be anything else in her company. Thomas has been to one or two evenings – doesn't like to get too involved, but he knows his history.'

Silence slowly fell across the room as a young man dressed as a footman stood part way up the stairs. Looking wonderful in his double-breasted waistcoat, breeches and silk stockings, he cleared his throat and introduced the Duke and Duchess in a commanding voice.

Out of the corner of my eye, I spotted Joyce at the back of the room. She had clearly slipped in to watch. Joyce was known as a formidable woman who took no prisoners; there were colleagues who had wondered out loud whether or not she had ripped out her own heart with her talon-like fingernails, but those who got to know her discovered a pussycat behind the fearsome exterior, and she was as proud of the work of her colleagues as anyone at Charleton House.

The footman stepped back and the 8th Duke came forward to speak.

'Lords, ladies and gentlemen, the Duchess and I are delighted to welcome you to our home for what promises to be a most enjoyable evening. We always gain such pleasure from sharing our family's treasures with our guests, and tonight is no exception. It has been a little challenging to accommodate so many of you, but I feel we have been able to find you rooms which befit your status,' the Duke paused as the audience laughed, 'and we hope you have a restful night's sleep. Before that, however, our chef has prepared a magnificent feast for us to enjoy before you embark on a range of tours and activities. We also have a very special guest, Mr Charles Dickens, who will be entertaining us before the night is drawn to a close.'

There were whoops and whistles at the mention of the famous author.

'So please, take a moment or two to finish your drinks, and then our staff will direct you to the dining room.'

A polite round of applause followed and the Duke took his wife's arm, leading her back into the crowd. I watched as they approached Thomas and Annie Hattersley. Annie gave an awkward little curtsy, and then appeared to hang on every word the Duchess said. Thomas took a step back and avoided getting drawn in.

I was about to head into the kitchen and check on Gregg when we were joined by Douglas Popplewell, who along with Mark would be leading tours during the evening. He had a scowl etched on his face.

'I hope she ends up in your group, I don't want to be anywhere near that woman.'

Mark offered him some advice. 'I'll see what I can do, but don't let it get to you. It might have been the first time, but it won't be the last. Leading tours is like herding cats – some are easily pleased and will hypnotically listen to and believe every word, and some will hiss at you as soon as you put a syllable out of place. Just do your homework and be prepared for anything.'

Douglas huffed and walked off, plucking the sole remaining glass of champagne off a table. Mark shook his head.

'Like that's going to help.'

'What happened? Why's he so mad?' I asked.

'Our delightful Miss Clough writes a history blog. As well as articles about particular people or places, she reviews the attractions she visits, their customer service, cafés, and tours. Last month she came here for our new tour on the current Duke's modern art collection. Douglas was leading it and she tore him to shreds in her review. It was quite painful to read. We'll need to be especially careful tonight – she's a Charles Dickens nut and will be looking for inaccuracies.'

'Was the poor review of Douglas deserved?'

'Some of it, yes. The review was a bit over the top, but that's her style. She once described me as an extremely knowledgeable maypole whose main fascination is the sound of my own voice.'

'That's so unfair, you're the epitome of shy and retiring.'

'Exactly. If I had my way, I'd tuck myself in the corner of a library and have as little contact as possible with my fellow man.'

I laughed out loud. As ludicrous statements went, that one rated pretty highly.

Dinner was to be served in the Library Café. As the name suggests, it resembles a library fit for a family as significant as the Fitzwilliam-Scotts. The walls are lined with books; during the day, leather wing-backed armchairs are scattered about, with a few of them gathered around a surprisingly realistic fake log fire. Tables and chairs of various shapes and sizes, all in dark wood, fill the rest of the space, giving visitors a warm, cosy room in which to enjoy tea and scones or a sandwich as they recharge their batteries before heading off to explore more of the house.

Tonight, however, we had turned it into a dining room appropriate for guests of the 8th Duke and Duchess of Ravensbury. Three long tables filled the space, each decorated with candelabras and autumnal-themed foliage from the gardens. Ivy had been draped along the centre of the tables, red rosehip berries glistened amongst the leaves. The coffee and antique pink shades of dried hydrangeas gathered beneath the candles. Box, yew and fir gave a nod to Christmas that lay just around the corner. An array of cutlery had been laid out, although it was silver plated, rather than the antique silver that the current Duke and Duchess used when entertaining. The log fire was roaring and the faux candles flickered along the tables. It was a wonderful warm haven from the cold November night beyond the walls of the house.

Tina, my Library Café supervisor, was double-checking the tables and putting the chairs in place. Chelsea, one of my young and enthusiastic assistants, was laying out a set of cards in each place. They were both dressed in black shirts and long black skirts, a long white apron and white maidservant's cap finishing off the outfit. I realised just how strange it was to see them in anything other than modern dress.

I picked up a couple of the cards that Chelsea had laid out and took a look. Gregg had asked for little recipe cards so that the guests could recreate their meals at home, but there were a few extras that I knew we weren't serving: a large pork pie, and chestnut and apple mince pies. There was also a recipe for a gin punch, something that Gregg had told me was a favourite of Charles Dickens, but we'd decided there was already enough alcohol available this evening and we didn't want to find ourselves protecting the contents of the house from a bunch of inebriated partygoers who wanted to clamber over furniture to take the perfect selfie. The guests would also receive a decorated

copy of the full menu as a souvenir, which contained extra information about Victorian dining at Charleton House.

I could hear a low murmur from beyond the door; it gradually
got louder and was joined by footsteps and laughter. The guests
were on their way, and I had yet to see Gregg.

'All set?' I asked Tina.

'Of course,' she replied confidently before shouting, 'Gregg,
they're here.'

Gregg stuck his head out of the kitchen door.

'Hi, Sophie, I'm ready. I'll just change my outfit. Are you three
okay to seat them? The wine is on the side and ready to be
poured.' Chelsea had a wine bottle in her hand before he had
finished speaking.

The doors flew open. The footman and an identically dressed
colleague held them and the crowd poured in. The cacophony of
sound increased in the confined space of the café as people
debated where they were going to sit. Chelsea and Tina started to
make their way around, offering red or white wine; menu cards
were read and discussed; guests called to one another across the
room; laughter bounced off the walls. This was a lively crowd,
and we were going to have to make use of our very best skills of
persuasion.

3

*G*regg emerged from the kitchen. And looked around the room nervously. It had taken me a while to convince him to say a few words to the group about the menu and I wondered how on earth he was going to cope with the excited chatter. He wasn't exactly shy, but he certainly didn't seek out the limelight and I knew he'd much rather be tucked out of sight in the kitchen.

His outfit was a little different to usual and I recognised it from old photos I had seen of kitchen staff at work in the 1860s. He wore the recognisable double-breasted white jacket of a chef. An apron was tied around his waist and he wore black trousers. On his head he had a white cap, a sort of loose bonnet that reminded me of a Scottish tam o' shanter. He didn't look wildly different from the chefs that could be seen on TV today, but his clothing was different enough to make you look twice at him. He was thin and angular, and his outfit seemed a little too large, like most of his day-to-day clothing.

'Ladies and gentlemen... Ladies and gentlemen, welcome...' Gregg's voice drifted off as he realised he was getting nowhere.

'LADIES AND GENTLEMEN!' bellowed Mark. He was

clearly well practised at getting the attention of large groups; the noise quickly dropped and people started shushing one another. 'Pray silence for Gregg Danforth. As well as preparing this evening's meal, he regularly cooks for the Duke and Duchess – the current Duke and Duchess, that is – and the variety of celebrities and dignitaries who join them in their beautiful home.'

Mark stepped back against the wall and Gregg was welcomed with a smattering of applause.

'Thank you so much for joining us this evening. I've had a great deal of fun poring through old recipe books and researching the dining habits of our Victorian forebears. In the end, I decided to take my inspiration from Charles Dickens, who will be reading to you later. Many of the dishes you'll enjoy are taken from or influenced by the food that appears in his works. For example, in *The Old Curiosity Shop*, Nell and her fellow travellers enjoy a stew. Don't worry, I've made a few changes and you won't be getting tripe.' There were sighs of relief from the room. 'Scrooge sees French plums in a greengrocer's window...'

As Gregg continued to speak, Mark sidled up to me.

'Motley crew,' he observed.

'Don't be so harsh, they've made a real effort. Well, some of them have.'

'I'm kidding. They seem pretty enthusiastic. We'll have our work cut out trying to exhaust them so they'll go to sleep at a sensible hour.'

Gregg had moved on to describing the intricacies of dinner service and its change from *à la Française*, where diners helped themselves from large serving dishes laid out on the table, to *à la Russe* where the courses were served separately and brought to each diner at the table by servers. The change had occurred during the reign of Queen Victoria, who was herself a huge fan of Charles Dickens.

'Why were Harvey and Betsy so concerned about Philippa and possible fireworks?' I whispered to Mark.

'Ah, come with me.' Mark led me out of the café and into the stone corridor immediately outside. I shivered. 'We don't have to watch the hordes attack their food. Not long before you arrived here, there was a bit of a scandal, depending on how much you really cared. Our delightful Philippa Clough had an affair with Conrad Brett. You'll see him later, he's playing Dickens. Once news got out, his wife Lycia hit the roof.

'Somehow, Lycia managed to resist wringing her husband's neck, and after about six months of living apart, she seemed to have forgiven him and they've been giving the marriage another go. To all intents and purposes, they seem quite happy. Although she does work with him a lot, probably keeping an eye on him. There were a few tricky moments in the early days. Philippa still visits the house on a regular basis and is often at the events that Conrad and Lycia are working, but there haven't been any serious incidents. Yeshim's team know to keep an eye on Philippa, but it's something we're all aware of.'

From inside the café there was a round of applause.

'Come on,' I instructed Mark. 'He's finished, I need to go help.'

As we returned, Chelsea, Tina and Gregg were distributing plates of a steaming, rich oxtail stew with root vegetables. I gave them a hand and left Mark to wander round the tables, engaging people in conversation, sharing a joke with them and no doubt passing on some of his remarkable knowledge of the house and its inhabitants.

With the main course underway, I paused and surveyed the room. I watched as Philippa and her friends tucked in, Philippa and Annie chatting away while Thomas silently worked his way through his meal. He didn't join in with the conversation nor, as far as I could tell, was he invited to. He picked up one of the menu cards and read it, shook his head as he laid it on the table and looked vaguely incredulous. I could only assume he didn't like or agree with what he had read.

'They all seem happy.' Tina had a wine bottle in each hand. 'They're thirsty, too.'

'Well, let's make sure they don't overdo it.'

There was a shriek of laughter from Philippa, and Tina winced. 'I'll never get used to that.'

'You know her?'

'My brother does, she lives on the same street as him. I've been to a couple of barbecues and Christmas parties that she's attended. She's good fun, but loud.' She spotted someone waving his empty glass in the air at her. 'Excuse me.'

A couple of the women in the room were starting to look a little uncomfortable. They were the ones who had opted to go all out in their costumes and were now finding that their corsets were not conducive to eating a large, heavy winter meal. Two women were loosening the ribbons on the back of each other's dresses. It was a wise move; there was still a lot of food left to come.

Mark nudged me. 'It drives me nuts when they assume that corsets have to be cripplingly tight. There were some daft fashion victims back then, just like now, who suffered in the name of a so-called perfect figure, but most didn't. How on earth do they think Victorian women danced, played tennis, sang opera, even climbed bloody mountains? They haven't done their homework.'

I spotted movement at the door and looked over to see two of our security officers, Pat and Roger. Roger looked at his watch and whispered something to Pat before they backed out and disappeared. I knew I'd see them again later, looking for leftovers.

An hour later and dinner was over. A dessert of stewed French plums with Italian cream and Gregg's melt-in-the-mouth short-bread biscuits had been welcomed enthusiastically, and many had taken the option of coffee, presumably with the intention of staying awake as long as possible and not missing a moment of their time in the house to the inconvenience of sleep. Mark once again flexed his vocal cords and called for everyone's attention.

'Everyone on this table, and the first half of this table – as far as you, sir – you'll be with me for this evening's tour. Everyone else will be with my colleague, Douglas.' Douglas waved at the guests from the far side of the room, no doubt relieved that Mark had split the group so that he had Philippa and Douglas had a slightly easier ride as a result. 'And don't worry, we'll make a comfort stop before we get going on the tour. Now, please gather your petticoats, don your top hats and follow me. Let's push through our need for a post-dinner nap and explore one of the country's finest buildings. Tales of scandal and salacious gossip await you, and if you're lucky, we'll bump into the odd ghost or two. Follow me please.'

He gave his handlebar moustache a quick twirl between his fingers, spun on his heels and dramatically marched out of the door, a gaggle of red-faced, overfed, but still enthusiastic and excitable guests behind him.

With the lights back on, the full glare made the carnage of dinner look even worse than I'd thought it would. Squint and the room resembled the scene of a food fight. As Tina and Chelsea set to work getting the room ready for breakfast in the morning, I joined Gregg in the kitchen. He was plating up a couple of meals for the live interpretation team so they could eat them in the privacy of their breakroom.

'They've asked for light meals only as they're going to be doing the dance scene in an hour or so and they don't want to be too full, so there's salad, but I've put a couple of dishes of stew aside just in case. They can always reheat them later, they have a microwave up there. Do you need a hand?'

I shook my head. 'I'll be fine, I can take my time.'

I was about to leave, but my way through the door was

blocked by Pat and Roger, who had returned and were surveying the scene.

'Bloody hell, no one said this was a party for toddlers. Don't these people know how to eat?'

'It's not that bad,' I replied. Pat, who was overweight and permanently red-faced, was known for his dislike of events that he considered 'modern'. His uniform stretched tightly over his stomach and he leaned slightly back, like he was trying to counterbalance the extra weight he carried. His colleague Roger was a favourite of mine. He wasn't exactly skinny either and he clearly enjoyed his wife's home-baked cakes, and he'd never turned down one of the warm cookies I occasionally dropped into the security office, but he looked like an athlete when in Pat's shadow.

He winked at me. 'I think it smells amazing in here, Soph, I bet you all did a grand job. Now, we were wonderin', any chance of some leftovers? It's a cold night and we've got our work cut out keepin' an eye on you lot.'

He smiled, and I couldn't resist. We'd have sent them some food over anyway, but I was a sucker for Roger; he was like an uncle everyone was fond of. Pat, on the other hand, was still looking around with a slight curl on his lip.

'It's a bleeding nightmare, we're expected to carry out all our usual duties and we've got, what, sixty crazies in costume that could sneak off anywhere to keep an eye on. We should be paid extra for these sleepovers.'

'Oh, it'll be fine, Pat. Won't it, Soph? It'll go without a hitch with you around.'

That was it – Roger was getting cookies delivered to his desk this week.

'Gregg's in the kitchen, he'll sort you out.' I smiled at Roger, but made sure it had left my face when I turned to Pat.

· · ·

I set off down a stone corridor and round the side of a courtyard. Light from windows above cast shadows onto the cobbles that filled the space, my footsteps echoing as I walked along a colonnade. I passed doorways hidden in the darkness of the November night and jumped as a mouse ran alongside a wall. Stopping, I collected myself; the last thing I wanted was to drop a tray of food.

A sudden movement caught my eye and I watched as Romeo, the garden team's adopted cat, followed on after the mouse, disappearing into the shadows silently. At the end of the colonnade there was a waist-high black metal gate with a 'No Entry' sign hanging off it. I pushed it open with my hip and started up the narrow wooden stairs beyond it. It felt like the stairs went on forever, my legs telling me that I needed to take more exercise.

Back stairs like these, which were off limits to the public, fascinated me. Even as a child, whenever I was taken to a museum or gallery, my attention was always drawn to the doors that said 'Staff Only' or 'Private'. I would watch as members of staff let themselves in, wondering what fascinating job they had. I longed to know what lay beyond, what exciting project they were involved with. Now I got to pass through those doors, although I had to remind myself not to take it for granted and hold on to that sense of wonder.

On the second floor, beyond a white wooden door, was the breakroom. I backed in holding the tray to find the 8th Duke lying with his feet on a sofa, mobile phone in hand. Seeing someone in Victorian clothing using modern technology no longer surprised me, but it remained a source of amusement.

Against the wall behind him was an empty rail that earlier in the evening would have held the costumes that had been prepared for the live interpretation team. A tall bookcase contained dozens of history books, biographies, magazines and files labelled 'research'. A narrow tower of lockers for valuables had an ironing board propped up against it with a rather ancient looking iron next to it on the floor. The 'Duchess' was sitting at a small desk with her back to me. She was flicking through a magazine.

'Ah, perfect.' Harvey spun his legs off the sofa and got up, taking the tray from me and putting it on a coffee table. 'Betsy, grub's up.'

'I'm not hungry,' she replied, turning to face me. 'Thank you, I'll heat some up later when we've finished. Harvey, here.' She tossed a bundle of white fabric at him, which he unfolded. It was an apron and he put it over his costume. 'Get gravy on you and you'll be in trouble, I don't think any of us have keys to the wardrobe tonight if we need clean spares. And don't overdo it, you'll get indigestion.'

'Yes, Mum,' he mumbled as he took a mouthful of bread dipped in stew.

'How's it going?' Betsy asked me. 'They seem like a lively crowd, the dancing should be fun.'

I was about to reply, but Harvey spoke before I had the chance. 'Hopefully they didn't have too much wine with dinner, otherwise it'll just be carnage.' He shook his head and looked at me. 'Some of the ladies can get a little handsy.'

'Where are the others?' I asked. 'Do they want any food saving?'

'On their way,' Harvey replied. 'They'll be here in about twenty minutes.'

Betsy looked concerned. 'That's cutting it fine. How do you know anyway?'

'Lycia messaged me.' He paused. 'She was checking how it was going so far.'

'Did she want to know if *she* was here?'

'Nope, didn't mention her. I don't think she cares anymore.' I knew they were talking about Philippa, who was sounding more and more like the star of the show.

'Well, she better behave herself.'

'Philippa or Lycia?' Harvey asked, sounding a little irritated.

'Both of them.'

'None of it was Lycia's fault. How did you expect her to react when she discovered her husband was sleeping with Philippa?'

'Slept,' Betsy corrected him, 'it was just the once, not that that excuses it. It's really none of my business.'

It was none of my business either and I was starting to feel like a spare part.

'I should go, but there's plenty of food left if anyone does want more. Yeshim will know where to find me if I'm not around.'

'Thank you,' they both chimed. I was quite pleased to get out of there. Betsy didn't seem too bothered by Conrad's affair, but Harvey had shown signs of having a pretty firm opinion. It seemed that drama was more than just the day job for some of the team.

4

I ran into Yeshim as I made my way back to the Library Café.

'I'm going to wait for the tour groups up in the Great Chamber, want to join me?'

I followed her through half-lit corridors, listening to her radio crackle from its position on her belt. It was business as usual elsewhere in the house and we could hear the security team locking up the parts of the building we wouldn't be using. Yeshim seemed to have fully recovered from the earlier shock of Douglas's childish games. I asked her whether that was characteristic.

'Sort of, he certainly likes attention. I heard that when Edward Flanders left, he applied for his job, and not just for the experience of applying; he really thought he could get it. It was a remarkable display of arrogance.'

Dr Edward Flanders had been a curator at the house and a minor TV celebrity, until he had been charged with the murder of a colleague. Shockwaves from the event had been felt deep within the Fitzwilliam-Scott family, as he was married to the Duke's younger sister.

'Douglas has no relevant experience; he loves history, but that's not enough. If I'm honest, I think he was attracted by Edward's TV work, that's what he really wants. Did you know about his book?'

'No, I don't know anything about him, except what I'm learning tonight.'

We had arrived in the Great Chamber. It was a large room with a dark-wood floor. The walls were covered in oak panelling and ornately carved lime wood displaying animals and plants that appeared to be tumbling down, so rich were they in number and detail. The large marble fireplace, normally filled with ornate vases, stood empty; the conservation staff had been concerned about potential damage and moved them for safekeeping like nervous parents before their teenager's first house party.

Yeshim and I sat on one of the large, low windowsills, our backs to the view of the courtyard I had walked around earlier. The windowsill was made of a light grey polished Derbyshire limestone revealing hundreds of fossils captive within it. It was cold to sit on and I regretted our choice, but Yeshim didn't show signs of noticing. I assumed this was where the next part of the evening's entertainment would take place. The room was more than big enough to hold a dance for sixty people.

I removed my glasses and gave them a polish on my shirt while I listened to Yeshim.

'I have no idea how he got a publishing deal, I can only assume he played on the name of the house. I can't quite pin him down on what the book's about, he's a bit evasive.'

We were interrupted by the arrival of Mark. Followed by his half of the group, he looked like the Pied Piper of Hamelin.

'We're almost at the end, ladies and gentlemen, and then you can have a quick comfort break before we head into the next part of the evening's schedule, but first I want to show you something that very few visitors know about. They certainly don't spot it unless one of us points it out to them.'

He made sure the guests had all come into the room, and then gathered them into a group just in front of the door, pointing to a piece of artwork above the frame.

'This shows the *Flaying of Marsyas*, a satyr, or nature spirit, who challenged the god Apollo to a musical contest. It was painted in the early 1700s. Marsyas is the one tied to a tree with his right hand above his head. Now, look closely. Can any of you see anything out of place?'

There was silence as the group peered at the painting. A few pointed at it, whispering to the person next to them.

A man in the group shouted out his answer. 'The watch! He's wearing a watch.' The group peered again.

'Where?' someone called out. Smiling, Mark stepped forward.

'Well done, yes. The right wrist of Marsyas. Can you all see it? Where there should be a rope binding is actually a wristwatch.'

The group members started to chatter to one another

'Ooh yes… There it is… I see it… Can you see it…? Where? Oh yes… Why…? Is the painting a fake?'

Mark started to talk again and the group quietened down to listen.

'Well, the theory is that it's a joke added by a cheeky restorer in the 1950s. Now you can point it out when you visit the house with friends, they'll be very impressed.'

A strident voice rang out from Mark's group. 'Appalling, why were they allowed to get away with it? It's not something to be made light of.'

Mark chose to ignore Philippa's remarks. 'If any of you would like to make use of the bathrooms, they are through this door. If you can then return to this room, we will await the other half of the party.'

Some of the group headed through the door, which led to a short corridor with a dead end. Other than to the toilets, they couldn't go anywhere, so we could relax.

Mark came over and joined us.

'How did it go, maestro?' I asked.

'Good. They laughed at my jokes; no one set any alarms off; I finished with the same number of people I started with.'

'Did they really laugh at *all* your jokes?' Yeshim asked with an exaggerated raise of her eyebrows. 'Really?'

'They did. Well, alright, almost all of them, but I blame the wine. It dulled their senses.'

'Is Douglas behind you?' I asked.

'You really don't know him, do you?' Mark replied. 'He's always running late, loves the sound of his own voice too much. What do you reckon, Yeshim, fancy a bit of a wager? I reckon he'll be fifteen minutes late.'

She appeared to be thinking. 'My money's on ten, but once we hit the five-minute mark I'll go and stand behind his group and make impatient faces at him. We're on a tight schedule.'

'I'll go,' I offered. 'I'd like to see him at work, plus he's bound to be telling them something I don't know and I want to keep learning.'

Mark stood up with me. 'I'll join you.'

'Won't that distract him?' I asked.

'If my presence distracts him then he's not much of a guide. We've attended each other's tours in the past and I trained him to deliver the Intro to Charleton House tour, so he's used to having me around. Come on, let's go find him and rescue his group.'

We found them in a wide corridor. Douglas was standing in front of a large window, his group had formed a semi-circle around him, and he was in the middle of a dramatic recreation of a duel that had occurred in the gardens over 200 years earlier. Unusually it had taken place between two women and was referred to as the Charleton Petticoat Duel.

I loved the story, a display of 18th century girl power. The elder sister of the 5th Duke had taken offence at a comment that a cousin had made about her age, claiming she was over sixty, when in fact she was not yet thirty. Both women fired their pistols, but neither had been hit. Next, they decided to resort to swords and moved to the courtyard below the room we were standing in. The cousin received a minor wound to her hand, but it had the desired effect and she agreed to write a letter of apology. It's said the swords used are somewhere in the Charleton House collections, but no one knows where exactly.

It was a story I had heard before, or I thought I had. As Douglas told it, two of the Duke's sisters were quarrelling and one lost a finger. I looked at Mark, a little confused. He turned to face me and grimaced.

'See what I mean?' he whispered. 'I bet even you could get that story right – you remember what I told you?'

I nodded. 'Cousins?'

'Yep. But he doesn't listen and I would guarantee he doesn't refresh his memory before delivering a tour. I'll have a word tomorrow.'

I looked over at Thomas Hattersley, who hadn't seemed worried about being in a different group to Annie and Philippa. He was shaking his head, sighing and glancing out of the window as though he had somewhere better to be. Something told me that Mark and I weren't the only ones to have spotted the inaccuracy in Douglas's retelling of history.

Douglas wrapped up his story and we stepped back as he led his guests through to the Great Chamber to join the rest of the group. He grinned at us as he walked past and gave us a thumbs up. Mark offered him the most exaggerated, cheesy thumbs up I had ever seen in response. I kicked his foot, but Douglas didn't seem to notice the obvious sarcasm.

By the time we arrived back in the Great Chamber, the 8th Duke and Duchess were once again mingling with the group. This time, they had been joined by a couple of 'friends': two more live interpreters we had yet to see during the evening. One was dressed as a handsome nobleman in a close-fitting maroon waistcoat and long black tailcoat. By his side was a young woman with blonde hair in a beautiful maroon dress that perfectly matched the waistcoat. The dress had a line of bows running down the back of the fabric that projected out behind her. They made an eye-catching couple.

This time, the Duchess addressed the group. She was excitable, unable to keep still, and clasped her hands together, giving a little clap from time to time.

'No event is complete without music and dancing, it's my favourite part of any evening. Now, I'm sure that many of you attend such dances on a regular basis – you are, after all, some of the finest members of society we've ever had the pleasure of welcoming here at Charleton. However, a little reminder does no harm. So, my husband and I, along with our good friends,' she indicated the couple in maroon outfits, 'the Marquess of Chelmorton and his wife, Lady Catherine, will guide you through some rather simple steps. We also have other friends here this evening who will assist.'

A couple stepped out from the crowd. They were beautifully dressed and wouldn't have looked out of place on a film set.

'Plants?' I asked Yeshim.

'Not exactly, they're paying guests like all the others, but they're friends of Betsy's and they know what they're doing.'

'My dear,' the Duchess turned to the Duke, 'would you be so kind as to ask the musicians to begin?'

There were, of course, no musicians; rather, another set of speakers was tucked out of sight, and Yeshim held a discreet remote control. The audience laughed as the Duke stuck his head out of the door and called to the 'musicians' to strike up.

A space was cleared and the six dancers took their places,

looking ready to start when a door burst open and a bearded Victorian gentleman with a book under his arm rushed in.

'Wait for me, please wait. I heard you were about to start dancing and you know how much I enjoy a quadrille. Please let me join you.'

Charles Dickens had arrived.

5

'My dear Charles, you're early.' The Duke and Duchess rushed over and welcomed him warmly, the crowd responding with sounds of recognition, some laughter and a little gentle applause. The Duchess held Charles's arm firmly and walked him over to the group.

Like many of the men in the room, he wore a black tailcoat, beneath it a rather cheerful waistcoat with broad purple stripes, and his trademark straggly beard. Mark had taken great pleasure in showing off his facial hair knowledge, telling me it was a grown out door knocker beard, and ever since then I had imagined Dickens's face attached to my front door. His cheeks and jaw were clean shaven, his hair slightly long and wavy at the sides. Conrad Brett clearly went to great personal lengths to ensure that he looked the part, although he appeared to be in his mid-forties, about ten years off the age Dickens would have been at the time tonight's event represented.

'Ladies and gentlemen, it is my honour to introduce you to our good friend, Mr Charles Dickens.' The group applauded and Dickens made a small bow. 'We were just about to remind our friends here of the steps to the Sir Roger de Coverley. Would you assist and join our little demonstration?'

'Of course, of course. Nothing would give me more pleasure. Would you mind if my companion joins us? She's a marvellous dancer.' He turned back towards the door where a young woman was waiting. She walked towards the group. 'Your Grace, please meet Miss Ellen Ternan.'

This was the first time we'd been introduced to this character, who I knew was Dickens's mistress towards the end of his life, and the woman playing her had to be Lycia Brett, wife of Conrad. Lycia looked about ten years younger than her husband, which still made her fifteen years too old to play Dickens's mistress.

The Duchess approached her. 'You're most welcome, please, do join us. We were about give a little demonstration of the Sir Roger de Coverley. Shall we?'

She stepped out into the middle of the room once more and the small group of experienced dancers followed. Charles handed his top hat to a member of the audience and joined the others as they formed two lines of four, facing one another, and the music began. They moved with well-practised ease to the sound of the flute, violin and piano, and as the wider group merged into the background of my vision, it started to feel as if I was getting a glimpse of the past. I knew that the real Charles Dickens had visited Charleton House and had performed a reading of some of his books. He had become friends with the Duke, who was a keen supporter of the arts, and they'd had a number of friends in common.

As the dancers smiled and laughed and threw themselves into the movements, the group clapped along. Some were intently studying the feet of the dancers and moving their own very slightly in an attempt to recreate what they were watching, while others started to look nervous. Some edged closer to the front, chomping at the bit to take part. I noticed a couple of the men who had shown signs of attending reluctantly slip towards the back of the crowd. There was no way we would get them up and dancing.

'That looks exhausting.' I jumped; I hadn't seen Joyce come in.

'You're here late,' I noted.

'I decided I'd stay to catch up on some work.'

'You brought your dancing shoes, Joyce?' Mark had wandered over to join us.

'Don't be ridiculous, you won't find me throwing myself around a room, and most definitely not if there is an audience.'

'Come on, don't be such a spoilsport. I admit you might be better off removing those shoes, but you'd look very dainty whirling around on your tippy toes.' Joyce's leopard-print shoes matched her skirt and scarf. The gold sweater she had paired them with made her a definite contender should any vacancies arise at a zoo. She looked ready to party, just not at this party. 'Or are you afraid we'll discover the true extent of your two left feet? Is the Lady Joyce worried about dropping down a peg or two in our estimation?'

Joyce let out a puff of air. 'I'll have you know that my mother was a Tiller Girl. I can high kick with the best of them.'

Mark looked as stunned as I felt. I immediately pictured Joyce in a glittery leotard, with tall feathers on her head, her legs going, well, all the way up. I could tell Mark was doing the same. Joyce looked between the two of us as we stood in silence, a faraway look in Mark's eyes that mine no doubt reflected.

'Stop it, both of you, I know what you're doing. And for the record, I would still look incredible in shimmer tights and a feather boa.'

'I hope you'd wear more than that,' Mark replied, a little shocked. 'Come on, give us a demo. I'm sure Roger de Coverley wouldn't mind you adding a modern touch to his moves. Pleeease,' he begged.

Joyce was saved as a round of applause refocused our attention and we watched the Duke and Duchess split the large group into lines. They knew better than to ask the men skulking at the back more than once. A couple of women sat it out too, taking a seat on the windowsills. The rest of the group milled around, finding their places until they were lined up in a number of rows, ready to start taking instructions. Yeshim had joined the Duke as controlling the music was going to take a bit more focus.

'So...' Mark was edging round a subject, '...are you going to tell us why you didn't end up strutting your stuff on the stage of the Folies Bergère or the London Palladium? Can you imagine how high my gay street cred would have rocketed if it was known that I was friends with a Tiller Girl?' He looked playfully disappointed.

'I am sorry for shattering your dreams and sending you into social status poverty. If I have the chance to do it all over again, I'll ensure you are at the forefront of my decision making.'

'Thank you, Joyce,' he replied, 'I would appreciate it.'

'I was far too interested in boys,' she continued. 'Sadly I was too young to know just how much work was required for so little return when it came to the opposite sex.'

I wasn't sure Joyce had ever learnt that. Three ex-husbands and a number of failed affairs hadn't dimmed her enthusiasm for finding Mr Right, even in her... well, none of us are sure which decade Joyce is in, but I'd guess at least her sixth.

As I turned my attention back to the dancing, I watched as Douglas was persuaded to join in. He pretended to resist, and then succumb to the charms of the Duchess. He was positioned opposite Philippa Clough and his expression travelled from laughter, to surprise and recognition, and then to deep annoy-ance. A hard look set on his face, and his bow to her appeared to be delivered with deep reluctance. Philippa smirked, and then threw herself into the music. Her over-the-top enthusiasm served her well and made Douglas look like a miserable, sulking teenager.

'I can almost feel his pain,' Mark commented as he watched. 'I bet he's convinced his skin will burn every time he has to touch her hand.'

'Is that the blog woman?' Joyce asked. 'I heard about her dalliance with the charming Mr Dickens.' Her eyes were now following Charles Dickens around the room. 'I can't blame her, he is rather good looking.'

'And rather married,' I added. Joyce had been involved with a married man before, and it looked as if it wasn't necessarily off the table for the future either.

'Not happily if he's playing the field.' Her eyes hadn't left him.

'If the rumours are correct, they patched it all up,' Mark added, 'so allow your wandering eyes to wander elsewhere.'

'Are you telling me how to conduct my love life, Mark Boxer?'

'Oh God, she's used my full name,' he muttered. 'I wouldn't dare. Married men, men who live thousands of miles away, men who live in burrows, men who dance naked at the summer solstice – I will fully support your relationship choices, no matter where you cast your leopard-print net.'

'Good. How Bill puts up with you, I will never know. He deserves a sainthood.'

'He was rewarded this side of the grave when I married him.'

'I've had enough,' Joyce huffed. 'Sophie, keep an eye on him; he needs round-the-clock supervision and the baton has been passed to you this evening.'

I laughed as she tottered out of the room on her wedges while Mark screwed up his eyebrows and pouted.

'Bloody woman,' he muttered. 'Still, I'd give anything to see her as a Tiller Girl. The Grim Reaper could take me after that and I wouldn't mind.'

The dance was in full flow and most of the group had picked up the steps needed to muddle their way through. When someone stumbled or headed in the wrong direction, they were met with laughter and good-humoured shouts to get them back on track. Philippa's energy knew no bounds and she had moved on to resembling an overeager horse attempting to dance on ice. She was having a blast; those who received an enthusiastic tug or twirl from her, less so. Charles was met with the awe of a living celebrity each time he came into contact with a guest, although I noticed the smile briefly vanish from his face when the dance moves brought him close to Philippa. She seemed to remain utterly oblivious to her impact on those around her.

'This is a good way of exhausting them,' observed Mark. 'There's less chance of any of them rising at sparrows' fart and needing entertaining.'

'Sparrows' what?' I was getting used to Mark's odd expressions, but this one was new to me.

'Fart, sparrows' fart. Dawn. How did you not know that? Anyway, tire them out, give them some hot cocoa, smother the snorers in their sleep and you might get a nap yourself.'

'What makes you think I'm staying the night? I'm going to head home and snuggle up with Pumpkin before returning to make this merry lot breakfast.'

'You and that cat.' Mark shook his head. 'There'll never be room for a man in your life with her around, she's got you under her non-opposable thumb.'

Pumpkin, my overweight, domineering tabby cat was, if I was honest, the love of my life. She and Mark had a love-hate relationship that had got stuck on the side of hate. I was sure she'd welcome a man into our home, just so long as that man wasn't Mark.

'Excuse me.' I stepped away from Mark, having seen some movement through the doorway, and made my way onto the landing. The movement had been shadows and I looked over the balustrade. At the bottom of the stairs, the comedy pairing of Pat and Roger were dancing to the strains of music that floated out of the door. Roger seemed to be rather enjoying himself as he pretended to tango. Pat, on the other hand, seemed to be poking fun at the activity upstairs, doing an exaggerated effeminate walk and twirl before turning and repeating the move, his nose in the air and the curl of his lip still firmly in place. He stopped after only a few minutes, clearly having exhausted the limited amounts of energy he possessed.

'Bloody idiots,' I heard him mutter. 'Come on, Rog, let's leave them to it.'

Pat put an arm round Roger's shoulder as they walked towards the door.

'It's rather nice,' I heard Roger comment. 'I should take my missus dancing one of these days.'

As they left, I heard a mobile phone ring and watched as Roger answered it before they disappeared out of sight. I went back to Mark, questioning just how secure our crack security team would keep us if there was a problem during the night, and making a note never to deliver any more cookies to the security office if Pat was on duty.

Half an hour later and the dancing came to an end, the dancers looking particularly bedraggled. Ties were undone, corsets had been loosened and a few shoes had been discarded. No one could say that they hadn't thrown themselves into it with gusto. Those who had sat it out were starting to look bored; the timing was perfect to give them all a break and let the dancers get their breath back.

Bottles of water and plates of biscuits were waiting for the guests in a room off the Long Gallery; we needed to get them out of the way so we could set the room up for the next event of the evening. Warders escorted them out, and Mark and I watched as they wearily wandered, and in some cases staggered, in the direction they were led. Tired laughter echoed through the room and down the stairs.

Douglas accompanied a group of women who were hanging on his every word. 'I had a magazine article published last week, and my book will be released next year,' he was telling them. 'The manuscript is almost finished and I've been told that a TV deal will follow shortly. Of course I'm not interested in all the attention, I just want to be able to bring my love of history to as many people as possible.'

The women oohed and aahed like they were in the presence of a rock star. It seemed that Douglas had found some fans who were as impressed with him as he was himself. I was glad Mark had stepped away and not been privy to Douglas's comments; I didn't think his eyes could withstand rolling that far back in his head.

'Darling, you have got to be kidding.'

I turned and saw that the only people remaining in the room were Charles Dickens – Conrad – and his wife Lycia. Conrad was reluctantly defending himself.

'I only danced with her because that was the way the turns went. Betsy was placing everyone, not me. You know I can't stand the woman.'

'I'd hoped we'd put all this behind us.' Lycia stalked from the room. She didn't seem to have enjoyed the event quite as much as the others.

'We have, *I* have,' he called after her. As he followed his wife out of the room, I couldn't help but wonder if the sticking plaster holding their marriage together was becoming unstuck.

6

I needed coffee. It was 10.30 and I was starting to flag. I could have gone home, I wasn't really needed anymore, but I wanted to stay for the reading.

I knew that Dickens would be reading from a number of his books, including *A Christmas Carol* and *Oliver Twist*. Both of them were books that I had loved growing up after my father had read them to me when I was a child. My father had passed away a couple of years ago, so I was expecting to find it emotional, but I wouldn't have missed it for the world.

I didn't want to fall asleep during the reading, so I needed an injection of caffeine. I left the group to it and headed to my office, just off the Library Café kitchen. Once down the stairs, I took a shortcut back across the courtyard, round a few corners, and then into the stone corridor that led to the café. It was dark, the only glow coming from the kitchen where Gregg had left a light on, so I was able to navigate my way round and through to my office.

The tables were all laid for breakfast and the kitchen was cloaked in the smell of freshly baked bread. Gregg and I had agreed to bring the group back into the 21st century with a modern breakfast menu that gave a nod to Dickens. In *Barnaby Rudge*, a breakfast included Yorkshire cakes, similar to brioche, and we would fill the bread rolls with bacon. Another option would be *Oliver Twist* inspired gruel, or oatmeal with lots of additional fruit and nuts that guests could add as they wished.

Helping myself to a Yorkshire cake, I trusted that Gregg had made plenty extra, and then prepared myself a coffee. I took the slow option, making a drip coffee and enjoying some silence as the water travelled through the grounds. I freely admit to being an out-and-out coffee addict, finding the perfect bean close to a religious quest, although right now I was more interested in its ability to keep my eyes pinned firmly open.

Coffee is one of my favourite aromas in the world and I took a deep breath, closing my eyes at the same time. I opened them quickly at the sound of coughing. Peering through the window onto the lane that ran along the back of the house, I could see the outline of a slim male in evening dress, at the end of one arm the glow of a cigarette.

On closer inspection, I could see that Charles Dickens was having a quick smoke before his performance. It was surreal, watching the famous author pace back and forth outside my window. It didn't matter how well I knew the circumstances, it looked very odd.

I cooled my steaming mug of coffee with an indulgent drop of cream and enjoyed a few mouthfuls, burning my tongue in the process, then poured the rest into a travel mug. I wasn't allowed to take coffee into the main rooms of the house, but I decided to take my chances and break the rules.

With my mug in my hand, I retraced my steps through the shadows of the courtyard and along the colonnade. Half way along, there's a deep doorway that always unnerves me; its thick black shadows have the potential to hide a number of people, and I always pick up my pace as I pass it, just to be on the safe side. Ridiculous, I know, but I do it every time.

Tonight was no different, apart from the fact I could have sworn I heard whispers and the rustle of fabric coming from within. My pace quickened even more than usual and I practically leapt the last few feet towards my destination. But as I reached the bottom of the staircase I was aiming for, I stopped. It hadn't been my imagination. It's always been ghostly quiet along the colonnade – no breeze, no paper blowing along the ground. Nothing that would naturally create the noises I could have sworn I'd heard.

Too afraid to get up close and investigate, I found my own shadowy corner and waited. After all, if the sources of the noises were anything to do with this evening's sleepover, they would have to reveal themselves soon; the reading was due to start at any moment.

It didn't take long before a man and a woman in Victorian dress stepped out into the half-light. From a distance, they could have been any of the guests, but as they walked closer, I could see the high quality of their outfits. As they were about to turn into the stairwell, the man took the woman's hand, raised it to his mouth, kissed it, and then let her run on ahead. She was Lycia Brett, and the man wasn't her husband, Conrad; it was Harvey Graves, better known this evening as the 8th Duke of Ravensbury.

The Great Chamber had been reset while everyone was getting refreshments. Chairs had been lined up for the audience, and at the head of the room was a superb copy of the reading desk that Dickens would take with him on his travels. I had seen the Charleton Estate carpenter hard at work on it the previous week and he had done himself proud. It looked just like the one I'd spotted in photos as I read up on Dickens in preparation for the sleepover.

It was different to any podium I had seen. The desk looked like a tall box without side walls so the audience could see the movement of Dickens's entire body. He had been an extremely physical performer and it was important to him that he wasn't hidden. On top of the desk was a small, solid box, giving Dickens something to lean on to rest his arm during the two-hour readings he commonly gave. A little fringe of scarlet fabric decorated the top of the desk. Behind the desk had been hung a background of swathes of red fabric, matching the fringe. Dickens had been a showman, passionate about the theatre. It was said that if he hadn't been a novelist, he would have become an actor, and an excellent one at that.

The audience had taken their seats, the Duke and Duchess on the front row, Ellen Ternan towards the back. After a brief introduction from the Duke, Charles Dickens strode into the room. Dressed much as he had been before, he now sported a red geranium in his buttonhole, and he clasped a leather-bound book.

He took his place behind the desk, and all the photos and illustrations I had ever seen of Charles Dickens came to life before me. He spoke earnestly about the similarities between the work of a novelist and that of a performer on the stage. Then he started.

He began with the opening of *A Christmas Carol*. A mean and miserly Scrooge, he would screw his face up in dramatic exaggeration. The voices of the characters, each one different, were introduced to us, and it wasn't long before his body was as involved in the reading as his voice. He had huge energy, and over the course of the twenty-minute reading of select scenes, he took us from misery and crankiness to humour and joy. His audience laughed one minute and were terrified the next as a new ghost entered the scene.

The Duke and Duchess played their part, their exaggerated shock and surprise, laughter and delight encouraging everyone around them. At the back, Ellen's face was a picture of pride in the Victorian equivalent of a rock star who had chosen her as his mistress. I was brought to tears more than once during the event, and I spotted others pulling out a handkerchief.

Next he moved on to *Oliver Twist* and I knew we were heading for the murder of Nancy by Bill Sykes, always a favourite at Dickens readings. I found it hard to imagine that there was a single guest in the room who believed that the person before them on the stage was anyone other than Charles Dickens himself.

He was delivering the final scene when I glanced out of the window and saw one of the male guests in the courtyard, on his phone. He paced back and forth in the cold night air, his breath creating great clouds before him. I recognised him as Thomas Hattersley, who didn't seem too worried about missing the reading.

Douglas appeared behind me. Out of breath and flustered, he had just come up the stairs, although I hadn't heard him running. He didn't look happy and I wondered if he'd received some negative feedback about his tour, although his group had seemed more than happy earlier in the evening, except for the overcritical Mr Hattersley who wasn't really entering into the spirit of the evening at all. I wasn't sure why Douglas was still here; his responsibilities were over once his tour was finished. Mind you, Mark tended to hang around with me at events, so perhaps it wasn't unusual for Douglas still to be here too.

Yeshim gently took hold of my arm. 'They'll be done in a couple of minutes,' she whispered. 'Are the refreshments set up?'

I nodded. 'I'll come down.' Leaving Charles to the rapturous applause of his audience and about to begin a short question and answer session, during which I knew Conrad would never break character, Yeshim and I left the room.

A cold stone kitchen that would have been the domain of servants had been set up for evening drinks. Before leaving,

Gregg had prepared an enormous urn of hot chocolate. We had a jar of marshmallows, chocolate sprinkles and lots of whipped cream ready for people to make their drinks as indulgent as they liked. For those without a sweet tooth, there were all sorts of herbal teas and decaffeinated coffee. We didn't want anyone waking too early, or at sparrows' fart as Mark would say.

'Harvey must have been squirming.' Yeshim was talking as she spread freshly made cookies out on a wooden board. They didn't look bad; my afternoon spent baking 200 of the things had been time well spent.

'Why?' I wondered.

'He has started to be more vocal about wanting to play Dickens. Conrad has made quite a reputation for himself as one of the finest performers of Dickens in the country. He doesn't just work here; he spends a lot of time on the road, and Harvey wants a piece of that success.'

'Won't Harvey be given a chance?'

'Maybe. It depends on the event, and whether or not Conrad is available. Something like this, where the guests have paid a lot of money, we want to make sure that what we offer them is the highest quality, and that's Conrad. He always does Christmas here too, and that's a really important event for us. There's no way I'd let Harvey get his hands on that; he needs to go off and do more on his own, build up a portfolio, get experience. Right now, he's just grumbling.'

'What about Ellen Ternan? Having Lycia play her was stretching the imagination a bit. From what I read, Ellen was in her very early twenties around now.'

Yeshim gave a wry lopsided smile.

'Ah, well that's part of Conrad's penance.'

'His what?'

'After he slept with Philippa, and after all the fireworks were over, he and Lycia decided to give it another go. However, one of her demands was that she'd always work with him when he was on tour, and closer to home if there was even the slightest chance of Philippa showing up. That can sometimes result in a bit of imaginative casting in order to crowbar her into an event.'

'But couldn't she have played the Duchess this evening? Surely she was closer to Lycia's age.' It didn't make sense to me.

'True, but Betsy is playing the Duchess at a number of events over the next two weeks and we needed continuity. Plus there's only so far I'll go to accommodate the whims of a jealous wife. Having Ellen in the scene is a nice edgy touch, but most of the guests won't know who she is. It should impress those who are real Dickens aficionados as she's not often added to live interpretation events, so I was happy to go with it.'

'They're on their way.' Mark had stuck his head round the door. 'Prepare for the hordes and the quickest consumption of a plate of biscuits in living memory. Oh and, Yeshim, you'd better head to the Long Gallery. I think there's a problem.'

7

The Long Gallery looked like a war zone. Sleeping bags, camp beds, blow-up mattresses – the floor was covered in them. A couple of people were milling around, fetching toothbrushes and seeing if they could get an optimum spot near one of the heaters. Some clearly didn't care and had tossed their bags in a corner, happy to grab whatever bit of floor space was still available when the time came to go to sleep. A couple were standing near the door, bags in their hands, looking tired.

'We knew that the accommodation would be basic, but we didn't expect this. We thought we could cope with it, but we really need a good night's sleep. We were thinking we could stay somewhere else and come back for breakfast.'

Yeshim looked at me.

'Black Swan?' I suggested. The pub was my local and only a couple of miles from the house. 'You could give Steve, the land-lord, a call, see if he has any rooms free and if he'll wait up for them.'

Yeshim pulled out her mobile phone and took herself off to a corner to make the call, returning a couple of minutes later with a smile on her face.

'You're booked in. One of my team will walk you out and give you directions. Breakfast is at eight. I hope you get a good night's sleep.'

'They'll be the only ones who do,' muttered Mark. 'Apart from the snorers, of course, who will keep everyone else awake, but sleep like babies themselves.'

Philippa chose that moment to walk past, toothbrush in hand, and indicate towards the couple as they gathered up their belongings.

'They couldn't take it, eh? What did they expect, silk sheets and breakfast in bed? Some people...'

She walked out of the room with a look of disgust on her face.

Full of hot chocolate and biscuits, which had no doubt been devoured as if a plague of locusts had appeared, more guests were starting to arrive in the Long Gallery to get ready for bed. Some had chosen particularly outlandish pyjamas which they happily wandered around the room in. Others dashed from the bathrooms to their sleeping bags and pulled eye masks on, quickly blocking out the world around them. Toothbrushes were lost and found, toothpaste shared between strangers as people discovered they'd forgotten to pack any. One couple were still taking in the paintings, although most people were now too tired to care what hung on the walls above their heads. Yeshim spotted someone take a sip from a poorly concealed hipflask and went to have a word, and then reminded everyone that only water was allowed in the room overnight.

With a warder sitting at the door, a desk lamp next to him so he could kill time with a book, the lights were dimmed and we called out goodnight. The guests would have resembled an extremely large, poverty-stricken Victorian family in one of Dickens's books, if it hadn't been for the lavish paintings surrounding them, and the expensive sleeping bags keeping them warm. The three of us made our way downstairs, acknowledging the warder at the bottom. Along with his colleague upstairs, he would make sure any night-time wanderers found their way to the bathroom and nowhere else. The last thing we needed was for the current Duke and Duchess to be disturbed by sleep-walkers.

'I'm off,' declared Mark. 'I might just make it home before the clock strikes twelve.'

'Me too,' I replied. 'Where are you sleeping, Yeshim?'

'The Duke and Duchess have given me access to one of their guest rooms, so while this lot toss and turn on the wooden floor, I'll get a couple of hours' gentle sleep in an antique four-poster bed. Don't let them know that, though, there'll be a riot. Thanks for your help tonight, you've both been brilliant.'

I gave Yeshim a hug and turned to Mark. 'Come on, I'll walk you to your car.' I linked arms with him and we stepped out into the cold night.

'That went well,' I offered. Mark shook his head.

'I'm deeply disappointed, and although they don't know it, every one of our visitors could have had a much more memorable night.'

I was confused; I thought it had been a fun, smoothly run event.

'If it's the last thing I do,' he continued, 'I will see Joyce high kick her way through the can-can in a leotard and tights that have more glitter on them than any piece in Liberace's wardrobe. How did we not know this about her?'

I laughed. 'She's a remarkable woman, and I reckon there's plenty more revelations where that came from. Chances are she was a member of the Résistance during the Second World War and carried out more missions than any man alive.'

'That would make her more than ninety years old,' he stated with a furrowed brow.

'Correct. Do any of us really know how old she is? There's also the chance that she was part of a youth preservation experiment and is now well into three digits, yet has the physical function of a woman in her thirties.'

He laughed. 'I wouldn't put it past her.'

We'd reached the back lane. Roger was standing at the security gate, bundled up in an enormous coat, his nose poking out from above a scarf.

'You're off?' He didn't sound very happy, which was unlike the ever-cheerful Roger, but I put it down to the cold and late hour. 'I wouldn't want to be sleepin' on that floor. But if they're prepared to pay good money to…'

Before he could say anything else, his radio crackled into life. He listened, and then responded.

'Okay, I'll call Yeshim and she'll be right with you.'

'Don't do that,' I butted in. 'Let her sleep, she'll be up early with that lot as it is. I'll go.'

'It was the warder in the Long Gallery, apparently one of the guests needs to talk to a manager.'

I kissed Mark on the cheek and sent him home.

I reached the top of the stairs where the warder was waiting for me with a rather tired-looking man in checked pyjamas. Before the warder had a chance to speak, the man stepped forward. He was clearly on a mission.

'It's ridiculous!' he fumed at me. 'How the hell are any of us meant to sleep with that kind of racket going on?'

'I'm sorry, sir, but I'm not aware of the nature of the problem.' The door to the Gallery was closed and I couldn't hear anything.

'It's inconsiderate and shouldn't be allowed.'

'Sorry, sir, but I don't…'

'Snoring! Snoring like a freight train. There's two of them, one in each corner of the room. What are you going to do about it?'

It took all my self-control not to laugh. What did he think I was going to do? Smother them in their sleep?

'There's nothing I can do, sir. I know that everyone was advised to bring earplugs if they were light sleepers. They're entitled to sleep, and this is one of the risks when you spend the night in a room with a large group of people.'

'Well, I won't be sleeping. I have to work tomorrow and... and...'

He trailed off mid bluster, turned and stomped back into the room, the warder running behind him. I winced as the guest attempted to slam the heavy wooden door shut, but the warder caught it just in time.

I figured that while I was here, I'd go and check that everything, other than the noise volume, was okay. Creeping through the door, I smiled at the warder as he made himself comfortable back on the stool and picked up his book. I could see the man getting back in his sleeping bag, huffing and puffing as he did so, no doubt trying to make a point and ensure a few others suffered at the same time.

Everyone lay peacefully underneath the watching eyes of Fitzwilliam-Scott family members, who were wide awake on the walls around them. Then I heard it. I couldn't help but smile. The guest was right – they sounded like warthogs stuck in treacle. Two of them, competing from opposite sides of the room. I stifled a giggle and let myself out. It was time for me to get some sleep to the soundtrack of a snoring tabby cat.

The moon was casting shadows through the colonnade and I thought about my warm bed. Midnight had been and gone and I yawned, then jumped.

Something had moved. I'd yet to encounter a ghost, although I had been told there were plenty around, and tonight was not the night I wanted to do so.

There it was again. It was the black-and-white cat, Romeo, on another prowl. It seemed this was one of his favourite night-time haunts. I watched him dart in and out of shadows, and then vanish up a staircase.

Looking up, I saw a light on in the room above: the Fitzwilliam-Scott private library. It was part of the house that the public never got to see. If the lights were on, there was a chance someone was in there, and if the door had been left open, which was something the Duke was prone to doing, then Romeo might get in and give them a furry surprise.

As quietly as I could, I crept up the stairs. Romeo was nowhere to be seen. The door was closed, so I turned the handle, wanting to check it was locked. To my dismay, the door popped open, and almost immediately, Romeo snaked round my legs and vanished inside.

Damn, I wasn't going home any time soon.

The room was empty, the dimmed lights giving it a cosy feel. The walls were covered floor to ceiling in books; a sliding ladder that would run along the shelves was parked in a corner. Three well-used leather sofas surrounded a fireplace; a coffee table in front of them had books scattered across it. A beautiful wooden desk and matching chair were in front of the window that looked out onto the courtyard, family photos on display around the base of a Tiffany lamp.

The room had a masculine feel to it and I could picture the Duke in here on a cold evening, a glass of whisky in one hand and a leather-bound book in the other. I could easily imagine Dukes before him writing letters with a quill and ink, and hosting their male friends after dinner, while wives and daughters chatted elsewhere.

I scanned the shelves; I would love to spend a rainy day in here, the fire roaring, exploring the thousands of books. Sitting on one of the sofas, sinking into its soft, well-worn leather, I closed my eyes and rested my head back, imagining a gin and tonic in my hand...

8

'*S*ophie… Sophie…'

Feeling a hand gently squeezing my arm, I opened my eyes and found myself looking into the face of the Duke – the current Duke. It didn't seem right. I couldn't understand why he was there, waking me up.

'Sophie, you fell asleep.'

Then it hit me. Startled, I sat up and looked around. I was still in the library. My lap felt warm and I looked down at the black-and-white cat curled up there, fast asleep.

'Oh, I'm sorry, I'm so sorry.'

A smile crept across the Duke's face, and then he started to laugh. 'Don't worry. You must have been working late last night.'

'I was, it's the sleepover. I followed the cat and the library was open, he ran in and…'

'It's fine. Really, don't worry. It was actually the dogs that found you. Well, Romeo.' I looked over at the door where two well-trained black Labradors were patiently waiting for their master. 'They smelt Romeo and pulled me in here as we walked past.'

I was going to have to have words with Roger. The security

team knew the Duke was forever leaving that door unlocked and were usually pretty good about checking it on their rounds.

'They didn't want to chase him?' I imagined them both leaping on me in an attempt to get to the cat.

'No, they know him. He finds his way into the house from time to time. Before now, I've found all three of them curled up in one of the dog beds. He's part of the family, especially in colder weather.'

One of the dogs let out a quiet whimper and Romeo opened an eye. I stroked his head as he woke up, then watched as he leapt down, wandering over to say hello to his pals. He rubbed the side of his head against them and they sniffed him.

'Well, I should take them for their walk, and you... well, will you go home, or have you work to do?'

I was confused. Work?

'What time is it?' I asked him.

'It's 5.30. I like getting an early start on the day.'

'Oh God, oh, I'm sorry. Work, the sleepover. I should go. Thank you.'

He laughed again. 'Can I suggest that before you do anything, you make yourself a strong cup of coffee, and please, stop apologising. You've started my day with a smile. I just wish I'd found you earlier, I'd have directed you to one of our guest rooms.' He offered me his hand, I accepted and he pulled me to my feet. Face to face with him, I dreaded to think how I looked. Oh no, had I been snoring? Drooling?

'What should I do about Romeo?'

'Nothing, I imagine he'll come with us for a little while. Now, go and get that coffee.'

He gave me a warm smile and made his way over to the dogs and cat, the four of them looking quite the sight as they left the room. I stretched. My neck was painful after sleeping with my head back against the sofa for so long. My skirt was wrinkled and covered in cat fur. I made a conscious decision not to look in one of the large gilt mirrors on the wall as I walked towards the door. I didn't want to know what state the Duke had seen me in. Not yet, anyway.

The Duke was right, I needed coffee. Only I didn't need a cup, I needed a bucket of the stuff. I would head to the café, but first I decided I'd go up to the breakroom. I remembered I had taken dinner to the live interpreters the night before, but I'd never been back to collect their plates. It would save me a journey.

Sluggishly I pulled myself down and up various staircases and along corridors as though I was in some kind of dream state. I could barely function without my morning coffee. It was a good job I was already dressed, as that was something I couldn't be sure to achieve successfully without some caffeine coursing through my veins. I'd probably head to work looking like a clown, or Joyce!

I almost knocked on the door, imagining that there might be a half-dressed butler or 17th century Duchess in her underwear within. You never could be sure what, or who, you'd come across in this room. Then I remembered how early it was and just let myself in.

'Oh, sorry.' I had been wrong – someone was there. 'I just wanted to...'

In the dim light of a single lamp in a corner of the room, Charles Dickens was sitting at a small desk, his back to me, a top hat next to him. Still wearing the black tailcoat, his scarlet red necktie just visible over the top of the collar, he was slumped forward, his forehead resting on the leather-bound book he had read from the night before.

Stepping further into the room, not wanting to startle him awake – there had been enough of that this morning – I stood on the red geranium he had worn to the reading that now lay on the floor. It felt wrong; the whole scene felt wrong. His neck tie had never been scarlet. It had been crisp white, something the fashion-conscious Dickens would have insisted on. Now it was scarlet red with blood, the knife that I had brought up the day before on the dinner tray sticking out of his neck.

'Charles... Charles? Conrad?'

Silence. I backed out of the room and took my mobile phone out of my pocket to call security.

Charles Dickens was dead.

$\mathcal{P}$ at and Roger had reluctantly made their way out of the security office, where I imagined at least one of them had been snoozing at his desk, Pat telling me over the phone that I was making no sense at all and to wait for them. On seeing the body, they were suddenly very much awake.

'Don't get any closer,' instructed Pat, taking on an almost comical tone of authority as he flattened the already battered geranium under one of his boat-sized boots. 'Rog, get the police here. Sophie, we should leave Charles... I mean... well, we should leave him to it, and I don't want anyone stepping in that blood. Nothing's going to wake him.'

I closed the door carefully and quietly behind us. Charles might not be about to wake up, but it seemed the respectful thing to do.

Sundays are usually busy at Charleton House. Today was no exception, but not because we had visitors pouring in through the door. There had been no choice but to close the house; the police were buzzing all over the place and wouldn't be finished with their essential work until the end of the day, probably later.

After I'd found the body of Charles Dickens, or rather Conrad Brett, Roger and Pat had crawled into action. It was almost the end of their shift, but any hopes they'd had of getting off home to bed had been dashed, and the look on Pat's face had made it clear that I wouldn't be forgiven for some time. Roger just looked resigned to it.

Poor Yeshim had thought she was having a bad dream when I crept into her room after being quizzed by the first police officers to arrive onsite and woke her with the news. After asking if it was part of the live interpretation and if Charles Dickens was playing a trick on his hosts, she had leapt out of bed and within minutes was in a well-pressed suit, her hair in a tidy bun, and she was as alert as ever. How she did it without coffee, I had no idea, and it made me love and hate her in equal measure. She went off to talk to the police, and then find the best words to break the news to the roomful of sleeping guests, and I went to start preparing breakfast for everyone.

Gregg was already in the kitchen when I arrived.

'Up to your usual tricks, then.' He smiled, his eyes twinkling from beneath his long fringe before he tucked it neatly under a white baseball cap.

'I know, I know, Sophie's around so there's bound to be a dead body somewhere.'

He laughed. 'At least the local constabulary is unlikely to get its police numbers cut with you here, so you're actually helping with jobs. Then there's the undertaker, florists, caterers – you're a one-woman employment campaign.'

'There must be better ways to keep people busy,' I sighed, 'but I'll go with the positive spin. Now, how are we going to keep sixty hungry, sleepy, shocked people happy? We can't do the sit-down breakfast we'd planned.'

'Already sorted, boss. I figured we could do a huge pile of

bacon butties – that way if people just want to leave, they can take them with them. I'll have takeout containers ready for the gruel. I'll also do extra for the police and any staff that are onsite and involved. Can I leave the coffee in your hands?' He peered at me. 'Have you had any coffee? You haven't, have you? Don't move, I'm not letting you near boiling water until you've had coffee.'

I pulled a face at him. 'Hey, what do you think I do at home?'

'What risks you take in your home are up to you. We have one dead body already, I don't want to add a badly scalded one – yours or anyone else's – to the casualty list. Now sit down.'

I did as I was told and watched as he made me a coffee. Willing him to hurry up, I noticed Gregg was eyeing me up and down.

'What?' I looked for a stain on my skirt. 'What is it?'

'Did you sleep in that?'

I groaned. 'Is it that obvious?'

'You did? I was only joking, but I must introduce you to my friend Mr Iron, and what's with all the fur?'

As Gregg handed me my mug of coffee, I told him where I'd spent the night. He howled with laughter.

'That's priceless. No wonder you look like you've been dragged through a hedge backwards.' He kept laughing as he started preparing the Yorkshire cakes, handing me half of one covered with a thick layer of butter.

'Come on, let's get coffee to the masses before you get dragged away for more questioning and I have to do this on my own.'

After helping Gregg take three huge urns of coffee over to the stone kitchen that we'd used the night before, I returned to the Library Café and dismantled the long tables we had set up. People were going to be coming and going, so there was no point having it set up for a formal meal. As I quickly turned it back into the cosy café, made sure the faux fire was roaring away and put the leather armchairs in place, I had a quick flashback to falling asleep in the Duke's library and grinned. I wasn't going to be allowed to forget that for a long time, especially once Mark and Joyce found out.

The Library Café back to normal, I put on an apron and helped Gregg with the mountain of food that was starting to grow. Looking out onto the back lane from the kitchen window, we had a prime spot for watching all the police activity. Forensic teams in white overalls fetched a case from the back of a van, and I watched as Detective Sergeant Colette Harnby walked past, focused intensely on a phone conversation. I had yet to see my friend Detective Constable Joe Greene, but I guessed he would be interviewing the guests.

Gregg carried a platter of bacon butties out into the café as I heard the door open and Yeshim announce to the small group with her that they could help themselves and stay in the café as long as they wanted. A warder was with them and I knew he would escort people out when they were ready to leave.

Yeshim came over to me. 'A handful have been interviewed and have left already, some are being interviewed and others are on their way. Just keep the food coming. How are you?'

'Me? Fine, why?'

'You found the body. I know it's not your first time, but still...'

'Honestly, I'm fine. I didn't get up close. Has Lycia been contacted?' Despite the problems in their marriage, it would still be an awful shock when she found out her husband had been killed.

Yeshim shook her head. 'No, the police can't contact her. Her phone seems to be switched off. They've sent a couple of officers to their house. She's also due at work today so she'll turn up of her own accord at some point. We'll keep an eye out for her.' Her phone rang. 'It's DS Harnby, I should go.'

Back in the kitchen, Gregg was almost done. I stood at the window, watching Pat chat to a colleague and then walk towards the gate. The police must have finished with him and he was heading home.

A couple of minutes later, I watched as a tall, slim man in a dark suit strode along the lane. He looked out of place in a Victorian gentleman's tailcoat, his cream necktie undone and flapping in the breeze. There was a confused look on his face and he glanced about him as he walked.

'Oh my God,' I gasped.

'What?' Gregg dashed over. 'Have you cut yourself?'

'No, no, it's Charles. Look, it's Charles Dickens.'

Looking like an extra in a movie, Conrad Brett was walking down the lane. He definitely wasn't dead.

Joe picked up his mobile phone on the first ring.

'Good morning, Grim Reaper.' There was a lightness in his voice. 'I appreciate you keeping us busy, but can you do it on a weekday? I was planning on getting the motorbike out today, it's finally stopped raining. Will you put the kettle on? I'll be over in a minute to ask you some questions.'

'Joe, stop talking. He's not dead, I was wrong. It's not Dickens. Charles Dickens isn't dead.'

'Umm, I thought he died 150 years ago. People tend to die when you're around, not come back from the dead.'

'Shut up, Joe! The body – I said it was Charles, I mean Conrad, but I was wrong.'

There was silence on the end of the line.

'One minute, Sophie.' I heard mumbled voices; one of them sounded like Yeshim. 'Looks like we've just reached the same conclusion. They were about to move the body and Yeshim was asked to double-check his identity. It seems Dickens lives to write another day.'

'So who is it?' I realised then that it could have been one of a dozen men at the event. While the women could vary their costumes wildly with different colours, width of skirts, frills and hats, it was easy enough for the men to find a black tailcoat and a top hat and all look pretty similar.

'Thomas Hattersley. Yeshim has gone to find his wife with one of our officers. Apparently she's here and wondering where her husband has gone. Sadly, we've found him.'

10

I sat on a tall stool with my head in my hands, staring at my reflection in the metal of a kitchen counter. No longer paying attention to what was going on outside, I suddenly felt very tired. Gregg's hand rested on my shoulder and a mug appeared below my nose. He pulled up a stool next to me.

'Everyone's happy out there. We can forget about them for a while. You okay?'

'Yeah, fine.' But I didn't really feel it. 'I can't believe I didn't check who it was. I didn't want to get too close once I saw the knife and realised he was dead. Then Pat and Rog called the police and none of us wanted to contaminate a crime scene and... well, I'm useless without coffee.' Gregg nodded – my inability to cope without my first caffeine of the day is legend among the Charleton House staff. 'I just wasn't thinking straight. He looked like Dickens, he had the same hair, his book was on the desk, his hat, and who else would have been in the breakroom dressed like that? I should have checked.'

I took a long breath out and sat up.

'Well that changes things. I could have guessed at a few people who had a grudge against Charles, I mean Conrad, but I don't know anything about Thomas, let alone who might want him dead.'

'So you're already thinking about it, eh?' Gregg smiled at me. 'Lining up your suspects, working out their motives. I swear, it wasn't me.' He held his hands up in surrender. It wasn't all that long ago that Gregg had been wrongly accused of murder, so I was pleased he could joke about it.

'Yeah, you got me. I was thinking about it.'

'Goooooooood morning.' The kitchen door swung open and Mark waltzed in. 'Get the coffee on, we have a crime to crack.' Bill followed close behind. He rolled his eyes and mouthed 'Sorry' at us.

'How did you get in?' I asked. 'Isn't this place a crime scene?'

'I worked last night, so the police want to interview me. Plus security were distracted trying to keep the press at bay, and I'm married to the relative of one of the investigating officers. Add it all together and I'm almost as important as the Duke himself. Now, if you've finished with the questions, it's my turn. What *do* you look like? Did you sleep in that outfit?'

Gregg burst out laughing and stood up. 'I'm going to check there's still enough food out there, I'll make you both a coffee on my return. I'm assuming the urn isn't good enough?'

Mark screwed up his face in disgust and took a seat on the stool Gregg had just vacated. Bill gave me a hug and leaned against the counter. I was about to explain where I'd spent the night when the door burst open again and Joyce marched in. So much for the house being a crime scene, but then I couldn't imagine even a police officer having much control over Joyce.

'Right, someone tell me what's going on. Who's dead this time... Heavens, Sophie, did you sleep in that outfit?'

We'd moved to a table in the far corner of the café, away from prying eyes and flapping ears. Most of the guests were eating, and then heading home. There was no reason for any of them to stay, and it was only hunger and shock that were making some of them take their time. Every so often, another couple of guests would appear, loaded up with their overnight bags and costumes, grab some food, and then be escorted to their cars. Occasionally a police officer would come in and fill up a takeout coffee cup. Tina had arrived and taken charge, and I'd sent Gregg home. There was a strange atmosphere that made everyone talk in hushed tones – well, almost everyone. I'm not sure that Mark or Joyce are familiar with the concept.

'So, fill us in,' Mark demanded. 'I believe we now have the death of one of the world's finest authors on our hands. It seems rather appropriate that the man who wrote some of the most dramatic scenes to be found in a novel – think of when Bill Sykes kills Nancy – should die twice.' He shuddered dramatically. 'Shame he had to do it here, though.'

I tried and failed to get a word in to correct him. Joyce came to the rescue.

'Let the woman speak, for heaven's sake. You're not short of the overdramatic yourself, Mark Boxer, now quieten down. Sophie, you were trying to say something.'

'It wasn't Charles – I mean, Conrad. I thought it was, it looked just like him from behind, but I was wrong. It was another of the guests.' I looked at Mark. 'Thomas Hattersley. How well did you know him?'

'Blimey, I'd seen him at events, but I didn't know him to talk to.'

'I know him.'

We all turned to face Bill, who took another drink of his coffee. He was calm and collected, like knowing a murder victim was the most natural thing in the world. But then he was surrounded by some rather melodramatic people, so it was probably an unfair comparison.

We all continued to stare at him like he was a specimen in a test tube.

'What? We go to the same pub quiz, he was on an opposing team. He was good, too.'

'You're going to have to tell me more.' Joe had walked in and pulled up a chair, squeezing in between Joyce and me. 'So go on, then. I never thought your pub quizzes could help on a case, but fill me in.'

At first glance, the brothers didn't look at all similar, although they had the same soft brown eyes and their smiles were mirror images. Bill was an ex-professional rugby player with the broken nose to prove it. He was stocky and still looked to be made of pure muscle, with the exception of the little belly he was developing now he no longer played. I knew he went to the gym, but it wasn't enough to combat his increasing age and his love of good food. He was still very good looking, in a rugged way.

His brother Joe was taller. I used to describe him as being like a teddy bear, rather cute with a little extra weight on him, but since his move out of uniform as a police motorcyclist and into CID, he'd slimmed down. I credited it to the nerves and stress of a new job.

Mark had long been convinced that Joe had the hots for me. I had tried to dismiss it, but it was getting increasingly hard to disagree, and right now it was hard to focus on anything other than the heat of his leg against mine. But, I'm not looking for a relationship, as sweet and fun as Joe is.

'His team was always in the top two. To be honest, I think it was beginning to irritate some of the others who didn't stand a chance. I didn't mind, it's just a bit of fun. He was able to answer questions on almost any subject, but history, now that was where he was guaranteed to win.'

'What kind of history? Did he specialise?' Mark was clearly interested.

'Britain, Derbyshire, politics. I'd sometimes think he should have a job here. Only he could be dismissive if other people got things wrong or didn't have an answer. He wasn't very understanding.'

Joe was making notes, and without looking up asked his brother, 'Did he annoy anyone, have any fights?'

Bill thought for a moment, and then shook his head.

'No, he could be irritating, he was the kind of person to smirk when someone got a question wrong, laugh quietly to himself, but other than his team, he didn't really talk to anyone.'

'I'll need the names of his team mates before you go.' Bill nodded and went back to drinking his coffee. 'Do you remember him?' Joe asked me.

'Sort of. He dressed like a lot of the men, like Dickens. I didn't speak to him. He didn't look like he really wanted to be here; he went outside a couple of times and I saw him on his phone.' I felt myself start to go red; I still couldn't believe I'd been so wrong. Joe must have spotted the change as he gently nudged my leg with his.

'Hey, it's okay, it was an easy mistake to make.' He turned to the rest of the group and his voice returned to its normal volume. 'He was at the event with his wife, Annie. Yeshim told me that she's friends with a blogger, Philippa Clough, and they spent a lot of the evening with her.'

Mark glanced at me. 'After an evening with Philippa, he probably killed himself.'

'Well he'd have been pretty talented,' Joe replied. 'We need to wait for the report, but from first glance, the angle of the knife means there's no way he could have done that to himself. He was stabbed from behind.'

Joyce grimaced. 'Please, Joe, you're in the company of ladies. Do we really need the details?'

'Sorry, Joyce.'

'Clear fingerprints?' I asked. Joe shook his head.

'Clean.'

'What about his wife?' I asked. 'Surely she's somewhere near the top of your list.'

He shook his head again. 'You'd think so, but she takes sleeping tablets and slept like a log until everyone else started getting up. She has the packet of tablets, with one missing. Plus she's one of the few guests that the warders remember clearly for not getting up in the night. Unlike most of the others, she slept near the windows. Most people were on the far side trying to keep warm, but it seems she's the kind that likes to sleep with all the windows open, gets too hot otherwise. She was in the direct sight line of the staff member on duty by the door. She never moved. And she seems genuinely distressed – her mother came to pick her up.'

'But it was still someone at the event, that narrows it down for you,' I observed.

'Well yes, if you consider sixty guests and however many staff that were working "narrow". Plus you have a dark warren-like building where it's easy for people to sneak around undetected. You know as well as I do that a lot of the security here is smoke and mirrors. Your basic perimeter isn't too bad, and more cameras were installed after the murder at the food festival, but it's still easy to get around this place without anyone spotting you.'

'So,' I was thinking out loud, 'we need to determine what links Thomas had with people onsite. We can rule his wife out, but there's Philippa.'

I looked up to see three faces grinning at me, and Joe had 'Are you kidding me?' written across his features. He waited patiently to be sure I'd finished.

'Sophie Lockwood – and note I didn't say Detective Lockwood, because you're not – I'm beginning to wonder if there's a way of locking you in this café so you can't get involved.'

Mark laughed. 'Come on, she'd still solve it before you lot.'

That was below the belt and Joe looked hurt. I agreed with

Mark, but the last thing Joe needed was someone to take a stab at his ego. I felt bad for him.

'I could say that I'll stay out of it...'

Joe smiled. 'But you'd be wasting your breath. Just stay out from under our feet and keep a low profile when DS Harnby is about. She seems particularly tense about this one. Speaking of which, I should find her and let her know about Thomas. Thanks, Bill, I'll give you a call later and get a formal statement from you.'

Joe rose from his seat and my mind immediately started whirring, playing back the events of last night and trying to recall who I'd seen Thomas talking to during the evening.

'Now, girl,' Joyce tapped one of her long fingernails on the table in front of me, 'before you slip into Sherlock mode, you're coming with me. You look like the Wreck of the *Hesperus* and we need to make you look a little more like someone who works in Charleton House. You don't run a greasy spoon caff, you know.'

I looked down at the creases that had remained in my outfit and picked a couple of clumps of cat fur off my skirt.

'Come on.' Joyce rose from her chair and led the way, balancing perfectly on her pale green heels. They made me think of pistachio ice cream. I was rather nervous about what I was going to look like when she had finished with me.

Joyce's office was surprisingly tidy. It was normally packed to the rafters with containers and packaging, items that she'd been sent by people hoping she'd stock them in the gift shops, posters and cardboard displays. A huge box full of uniforms for her staff usually sat next to her desk, and there was always a mountain of paperwork that looked as if it was about to topple onto the floor. This time more of the carpet was visible than hidden and her desk was virtually clear.

She read the expression on my face perfectly. 'Spring clean.

Well, autumnal clean. Once the visitor numbers drop, I have more time to shut myself away in here and sort it out. Now, what have we got?' She pulled open a large cupboard door to reveal a wardrobe full of brightly coloured clothing. From a distance, it looked like a child's dream dressing-up box – Joyce has a rather striking taste in clothes. I was envious of the space. My office is so small, my only option is to hang my spare clothes on the back of my door. I was cursing myself for sending them all off for dry cleaning earlier in the week.

'I know you're a little more... subdued than I, shall we say, but I think this will do the trick.'

I held my breath; I knew I wouldn't dare turn down anything she offered me, but I was afraid of looking like an entertainer at a child's party. She held out a navy-blue pleated skirt. I was shocked by its simplicity, and just how much I liked it.

'Hardly wear the thing. I only pull it out when I have to give a formal presentation to the Trustees. Now, let's find something to brighten it up.'

It was hard to imagine the Duke and Duchess allowing Joyce loose in front of a group as important as the Trustees. I'd never known her not to speak her mind, but perhaps there were circumstances where that was useful. Plus she was never actually wrong, just less than delicate in the way she put things across.

'There we are.' Joyce whipped out a pink blouse with a large bow at the neckline. I couldn't quite make out the pattern and took a closer look. 'Tulips. A little spring-like for now, but everything else is too low cut for you.' She stared at my chest. 'You should show yourself off a bit more, you'd have a decent cleavage if you... well, shall we say, managed things a little better there.'

I groaned inwardly; I was never, ever, *ever* letting Joyce take me bra shopping. I wouldn't let her buy me a pair of shoes, let alone underwear.

'Go on, tuck yourself behind that filing cabinet in case anyone comes in.'

I quickly whipped off my crumpled clothes and pulled on Joyce's choice. I couldn't fasten the skirt at the back, but figured a safety pin would do the trick, and I'd just let the shirt hang out a bit to cover it. I twirled in front of Joyce so she could give her approval, or not. She laughed and handed me a pin from a pot on her desk.

'Ah yes, there is a bit of a height difference. That skirt is normally at my knee.'

I looked down at the skirt that was sitting mid-calf. At 5 foot nothing, I was hardly surprised that what on her probably looked like a sexy schoolgirl outfit made me look like a Sunday-school teacher.

'The blouse seems to fit.' I said the only positive thing that had come to my mind.

'Hmmm, yes,' she agreed. 'And that's probably the best we can hope for right now. At least you're free of cat hair and they don't look like you slept in them. Now, shoes…'

'No way!' I exclaimed. 'I mean, thank you, but I… I don't think we're the same size.' I stuttered out the best excuse I could think of. She ignored me.

'Try these.' She passed me some rather nice pale blue shoes with small heels. 'Wore them once and felt like a dwarf.' My feet vanished in them. 'Ah yes, I see what you mean.' She looked at my flat navy shoes. 'Well, at least the colour matches, even if you do look like a nun from the waist down.'

11

I couldn't remember the last time I'd felt more conspicuous. If it were possible to blend in with the walls, I would have done, but that was even harder than usual now that I was dressed like a child who wanted to emulate 'Auntie Joyce'.

I left the shop and walked across the Tudor courtyard. The cobbles were shiny and slick after a short burst of rain and I watched my step.

'Sophie? It is Sophie, right?' Betsy was looking me up and down. I decided to assume that her expression was one of admiration for my uniquely combined clothes.

'Hi, yes, that's right. Excuse the outfit, I didn't get home last night. What are you doing here?'

'I got in early to collect a few things, and ended up being interviewed by the police. It's just awful what happened.'

I nodded. 'It had been such a great event, you were all fantastic.'

Now that she was in jeans and a waterproof hiking jacket, she looked jarringly modern compared to the last time I had seen her.

'Thanks. It was fun, it's a good team and we work well together.'

Running into Betsy like this gave me an opportunity to start piecing together what had happened. Regardless of what Joe had said, there wasn't a chance in hell I was going to leave this one alone.

'I was wondering, what time did you leave the house last night?'

'Well, I got changed after the reading, and then when everyone was ready, we all had a drink.'

'We?' I asked.

'Yeah, the live interpretation team. We were a fairly small group, so we decided to hang around for a while. Conrad had a bottle of sherry for us to share. It was Dickens's favourite and Conrad wanted to continue the theme of the evening. A couple of us had bottles of wine that we took over.'

'So you stayed onsite?'

'Yeah, we were in that little art gallery near the entrance. There are sofas in there. Conrad stayed in costume and kind of hosted it. I never tire of him playing the role.'

'How did you all get in there? Wasn't it locked up?'

'No, it doesn't have a separate door, it's basically a large alcove off a corridor. We saw Roger from security, but he didn't seem bothered and let us carry on.'

'Have you any idea what time you all went home?'

She thought for a moment. 'I reckon about 12.30. It started to get a bit tense.'

'In what way?' I'd only been hoping to get some idea of timings and where people were, but this was sounding interesting.

She sighed. 'Well, once Lycia had got changed and joined us, Harvey started making comments about Dickens and his mistress. We all knew this was aimed at Conrad. Eventually the others managed to change the conversation, but then it got tense between Harvey and Lycia. Then Harvey stormed out and Lycia went after him. After that, none of us were in the mood. I went home.'

'Did any of you go back up to the breakroom?'

'No, not that I'm aware of.'

'Okay, thanks, Betsy.'

She smiled and left the courtyard. So, they'd all been drinking and tempers were running high. If Lycia and Harvey were having an affair, they were obvious suspects – assuming, of course, that like me, they'd mistaken Thomas for Conrad as he sat at the desk. The question was, which one of them would resort to murder to get Conrad out of the way?

I watched Joe escort a couple of guests past the security gate, and waited for him. He smiled as he saw me and walked over. I watched his expression change to confusion, and then to amusement. He was fighting to conceal a smirk as he reached me.

'Don't say a word,' I commanded.

'I wasn't going to say anything, I was just wondering when story time starts. You do work in a library, right?'

'A library? What is it about me? Why do Joyce's clothes make me look like I should be serving tea at a Women's Institute meeting, and on Joyce they look like... like...'

'Like she has questionable morals,' Joe finished.

'That's a bit harsh, but yes.'

'Because you have anything but questionable morals and your goodness is transforming the way we see the clothing.'

I laughed. 'You're full of rubbish. How's it going?'

'Slow. We're trying to piece together where everyone was throughout the night, and we haven't had the pathologist's report back yet, so we're still working within a really wide window of opportunity. Although logic dictates it was between 12ish and 5.30 when you found him.'

'I was thinking, Joe. When I first saw the body, I thought it was Charles... I mean, Conrad. So is there a chance that the killer made the same mistake, and the intended victim wasn't Thomas at all?'

'Yep, we're pursuing two lines of enquiry. Double the work, double the fun.'

That meant Harvey and Lycia could go on my list of suspects.

'Might Conrad still be at risk?' That had only just struck me as a possibility.

'He might,' Joe agreed. 'He's with Harnby now. No one would be stupid enough to try again while he's here at the house, especially while we're still swarming all over the place. But we might put an officer outside his house when he goes home, until we know more.'

Joe sounded confident, self-assured. He hadn't been a detective for very long, but he seemed to be finding his feet. I was proud of him, like a big sister would be. Maybe that was the problem – I viewed him more as a brother than a potential boyfriend. Perhaps the romance would come later, who knew?

'Sophie?' Joe pulled me out of my thoughts and I was grateful he couldn't read my mind. 'Sophie, I have to go. I'll drop by later.' He let his hand brush against my arm as he walked past me. I had to admit, he did look really good in a suit.

Back in the Library Café, I sat down in front of Mark, who was flicking through a magazine.

'Where's Bill?' I asked.

'Shopping. Apparently we'd starve if it was left to me. Supermarkets are just such soulless places.'

'He's not your slave.'

'No, no, he loves it. He's one of those people who will spend fifteen minutes comparing two different kinds of cheese, and look them up online to see what wine they'll pair with.' He shook his head, a look of wonder on his face.

'I doubt you complain much when that cheese and wine appear in front of you.'

'Never. Now there's a thought, is it too early for a drink?'

'It's 9.30, so yes.' Wow, 9.30. It felt more like the middle of the afternoon, but then I had been up since 5.30 am.

'Really, you look like you've had a head start on the alcohol.' He waved his finger in my general direction. 'Is Joyce responsible for this?' I nodded. 'I'm saying nothing.'

'Very wise.' I had expected him to pile on the jokes at my expense and was grateful for whatever had distracted him. 'What are you looking at?'

'It's a history magazine. I'm reading Douglas's article. It's surprisingly good. No mistakes so far.'

'That doesn't sound like him.'

'I know, but I guess if he's writing with all his research to hand, he has no excuse. If he's not bothering to remember it properly, then he'll struggle on the tours, so perhaps this is his forte. Maybe his book won't be so bad after all.'

'What's the article about?'

'Capability Brown, the landscaper, and the work he did here on the estate, especially the area closest to the house. Douglas knows his stuff, so he probably spent some time with the gardeners as well. He's got a real handle on the management of the grounds.' Mark had an expression on his face I'd seen before when he was carrying out his own research, or was buried in a book he found genuinely interesting. 'I might view Douglas a bit differently now.'

Tina had told me that the Stables Café had been overrun with the press. There'd been no reason to close the café that was housed in the old stable block a short walk from the main building – there would still be plenty of dog walkers who wanted a hot drink, and now there would be people who would come to gawp in the hope of seeing something gory, or watching a killer get led off in handcuffs. Then there was the press, and to be honest, I'd forgotten about them.

As soon as I turned into the courtyard, I could see that the café was busy. A few people were standing outside talking on their phones, a takeout cup in the other hand. Inside it was heaving and my glasses steamed up as I walked in. I'd made the mistake of leaving my staff name badge on and I was immediately faced with a barrage of questions about what I knew or had seen. I replied with the standard 'No comment' and walked quickly round the back of the counter. Nick, the café supervisor, looked pleased to see me.

'Sophie, what's it like at the house? Are the police still there?'

'They'll be there all day, and maybe tomorrow. How are you faring up here, are this lot giving you trouble?'

He shook his head. 'They're fine. When they first arrived, they were digging for dirt, but once they realised we weren't going to give them any, they settled down. Now they're just using us as a base. I figure it helps keep them in one place.'

'Okay, but if they start causing trouble or hassling the other customers, let me know and I'll get security over here.'

Nick looked utterly unfazed by all the activity around him. 'So long as they have coffee, they're fine, but thanks.'

I stepped back out into the cold.

'Do you work at the Manor House of Murder?'

'The what? Oh, very droll.' I rolled my eyes at the reporter and stepped around him. He wasn't going to have any luck with me.

12

*C*harles Dickens was sitting in the corner of the Library Café. His coat was hanging over the back of a chair and he'd removed his necktie completely. His unbuttoned waistcoat hung loosely open and he'd lost his geranium. Despite looking dishevelled and tired, he still managed to appear rather dapper. It was easy to picture him straightening himself out and within minutes having the other customers in the café enthralled with his stories.

I could see that his coffee mug was almost empty, so I fetched him another. He was miles away.

'Conrad? Conrad?'

'Oh, hello. Sorry.'

'I thought you might need another.'

'Thank you.' He took a swig, showing no signs of the hot liquid burning his mouth. Sitting back in his seat, he pulled out his overstuffed wallet and started to ease a five-pound note out. I waved it away.

'It's on me.'

'Thank you. I'm afraid I don't know your name.'

'Sophie.'

'Thank you, Sophie. I saw you last night. I hope you enjoyed it.'

'You were fantastic. I love Dickens.' He smiled weakly. I nodded at his waistcoat. 'Do you dress like that all the time?'

He followed my eye line. 'Oh no. Last night, I was… well, I guess I was distracted. I didn't go home.'

'I heard about your little party. I'd love to share a glass of sherry with Charles Dickens.'

He looked momentarily confused. 'You mean last night? Oh, it wasn't a party, not really. Certainly didn't finish up that way.' All the energy I had seen in him had gone and he just looked as if he needed to go to bed, but I guessed that he didn't feel much like going home if there was someone out there who wanted him dead.

I decided to push him. If he was tired, then maybe his defences would be down.

'Where did you spend the night if you didn't go home?'

'The Black Swan. I was lucky they had a room free.'

I was reminded of the couple who had done the same thing and gone to the Black Swan for the night. How lucky they were to avoid all the drama. I wondered if they had attempted to get back in the house for breakfast, or if they just hadn't bothered and had gone home.

'Are you worried?'

'What about, that someone is out to kill me?' He shrugged. 'Yes, no. It seems so ridiculous and the police aren't worried, but there is a man dressed like me who is now lying in a morgue, so I suppose I should take it seriously.'

'Do you have any idea who would want to kill you?'

'You sound like the police. No. I'm sure I've rubbed a few people up the wrong way, but not kill me, no. At least I hope not.' He stroked his beard, gently pulling it into a point.

'What about Lycia?'

A bark-like laugh burst out of him. 'My wife? Now I know

I've made her mad, but it wasn't that bad. Anyway, things are better now, or they were.' He stopped and looked at me intently. 'Hmm, my own fault. I guess my stupidity will haunt me forever and I have no one to blame but myself.'

'You said things "were" better?' Of course I knew what he was alluding to, but I wanted to get as much as I could from him. He sat in silence for a moment or two, staring into his coffee cup, then he started to talk.

'I thought we had it all sorted, I thought she'd forgiven me. I did everything she asked of me. I didn't take any jobs that involved travel unless she could come with me. If there was an event Philippa was likely to be at, then I would ensure that Lycia had a role so she could be there too and was visible. A sort of warning to Philippa, and me, I 'spose. I did it all, and willingly. I love Lycia and I kick myself every single day. I thought we were working it out, but I guess not. Harvey does a lot of work here at Charleton as well, so the more time we spend here, the more time they spend together. I know he's trying to win her over; I don't know if they've acted on it yet, but that's definitely what he's after.' He looked heartbroken. 'I guess last night wasn't short in irony.'

'What do you mean?' I asked.

'I was playing a man who has brought his mistress to an event, leaving his wife at home, and all the while my actual wife is thinking about running around with another man. He was probably trying to snatch stolen kisses in the shadows and alleyways of this place.'

I thought back to last night, and watching Lycia and Harvey emerging from the shadows. Sadly, Conrad was right.

'What about Harvey?

'What about him?'

'Do you think he would go to such extreme lengths to have Lycia to himself?'

'Heavens, no. He's classically handsome, I suppose, but that's all he has to offer. The ladies fall at his feet, but he's weak and insipid. He'd run a mile rather than confront the opposition.'

'Anyone else?'

'You make it sound like there might be a queue of people waiting to get rid of me. I'm really not that bad, you know.' He gave me a little smile.

'I'm sure you're not. But was there anyone else there last night who you've had a disagreement with? You're not aware of any strange behaviour? No one has threatened you, or tried to make contact with you? Sent you notes, phoned you and hung up when you answered? Anything odd that you dismissed at the time?'

'Only Philippa, but they were hardly threats. I was apparently the best thing since sliced bread.'

'How did she take it when you broke it off?'

'Broke what off? It was a one-night stand. A stupid, regrettable one-night stand. You think Philippa might have done this? A delayed response to it all?'

'Possibly. How has she been since you, well, you...'

'Slept with her? There were a couple of times she tried to make her way to our breakroom. I had to talk to Yeshim, and the staff were told to keep an eye out for her. We didn't want to make a fuss, just gently dissuade her from getting too close. Then of course Lycia was always with me, and boy can she give someone a good glare. That probably scared Philippa off on a couple of occasions. But after a while it all calmed down and Philippa just returned to being a devoted history fan and appeared to put her energy into her blog, which has gone from strength to strength. She's always here for events, and she has travelled to see some of the other stuff I do, but she's kept her distance. Some days it's actually quite nice to see her, a familiar face in a crowd, and I'm sure her glowing reviews have helped me get jobs.'

'So there's no hard feelings?'

He shook his head. 'Not that I'm aware of. It's Lycia that hasn't seemed able to let it go.'

Despite Conrad's confidence, I lodged the idea of Philippa
being involved firmly in my brain. After all, she had motive and
she clearly knew where the breakroom was. It wasn't impossible
that in the dim light, after a few glasses of wine and whilst in the
grip of passion and frustration, she had mistaken Thomas for
Conrad.

'What connection do you have with Thomas?'

'Nothing solid. He comes to some of the events, but not often.
I get the feeling he's dragged along by his wife. I've been pulled
into a few conversations with him when I was talking to Philippa
and I have lost my temper with him a couple of times when he's
pushed me too far, been disrespectful.'

I mulled over what he'd said.

'What are you thinking?' Conrad looked curiously at me. I
wondered if he could hear the cogs turning in my brain.

'I'm thinking I've not had enough sleep, or coffee.'

With a takeout coffee in one hand, and a bag containing a
chocolate chip cookie in the other, I stretched my legs in the
direction of Yeshim's office. She had one of the more attractive
offices amongst my colleagues. A repurposed bedroom that had
views of the garden, it was the perfect example of understated
elegance, rather like Yeshim herself. A large fireplace stood half
way down one wall, on top of it a display of the various awards
that Yeshim and her events team had won. The soft grey carpet
was spotless and the pale yellow walls added a warmth to the
room. Neatly framed photos of beautiful brides and handsome
grooms adorned the walls – happy couples who had tied the knot
under the watchful eye of Yeshim's team members.

The room smelt of delicately scented candles. I took a deep
breath in – pinecones and cinnamon. The smell of Christmas
which, it disturbed me to remember, was only next month. Three
of the desks were unoccupied, unsurprising for a Sunday with no

events other than the sleepover planned. Yeshim was sitting at her desk in the far corner, her legs curled underneath her and a soft grey blanket round her shoulders.

'Are you cold?' I asked as I put the coffee and cookie on her desk.

'No, I just find it comforting. Thank you.' She did a double take at my outfit, but didn't say anything. I spotted a pair of pink slippers on the floor beside her chair and she followed my eyes down. 'We all wear them round the office, gives our feet a break after walking around on hard floors all day.'

'Good idea, although I doubt health and safety would let me get away with that in the kitchen.'

She took a bite of the cookie. 'Still warm, yum. Thank you.'

'I think Tina was bored. She hardly ever bakes, but there's not a lot to do now. It's mainly just the police coming in to grab a coffee and get back to work. Have all your guests gone?'

Yeshim shook her head as she dropped crumbs onto the desk. 'There's still a few to get through. Harnby said she'd let me know when she'd done with them all.'

'I've got a question for you.'

'Of course you have.' She grinned. 'I'm rather disappointed you haven't figured out who did it yet.'

'I'm trying, give me a chance. I was wondering, you had a warder on the door all night? So wouldn't they be aware of who was coming and going, and who had left the room long enough to kill Thomas?'

'You're assuming the killer was one of the guests?'

'Not necessarily, but there were sixty of them.'

Yeshim pointed at an empty desk chair. I wheeled it over and sat down.

'We had a warder on the door and one downstairs. They were a point of contact in case there were any problems, and they made sure that people could find their way to the toilet without getting lost. But, it's a boring job in the middle of the night, cold too if you're downstairs. They're allowed to read and they were swapping posts so they had time to warm up. They also need to take toilet breaks as well. So, two warders isn't really enough, but we're running these events on a tight budget. Can I guarantee that no one could sneak out when one of them took a break, or they were distracted helping another guest? No. But having said all that, you'd be surprised at what they do remember. We also make sure that we have reliable staff working events like these – they're usually pretty on the ball, and over the course of the evening they start to recognise the guests. So, I can't guarantee it, no, and there may well be someone that slipped by unnoticed, but the warders will be able to remember a lot of things about many of the guests.'

'We didn't check the guests were all there when they went to bed.'

'You mean a head count? No. Maybe we should have done, but there's nowhere they can go that would cause any harm. Security lock the rooms we've been using once we're done, so the only places they could have gone are the cloisters and out onto the back lane where they'd be face to face with security.'

I thought about the open door into the Duke's library, but decided not to say anything if it meant that someone would get into trouble. Pat and Roger had a lot more to think about than usual with so many people sleeping over, and forgetting to lock a door only showed they were human.

'Does that help?'

'Kind of. It means there is a small chance one of the guests had the opportunity to kill Thomas.'

'But only if they knew where the breakroom was,' she pointed out.

'True, unless they followed him. Which is entirely possible.'

'We've not narrowed it down any, have we?'

'Nope, I just wish I knew more about him.'

'What about Joe? Can't he give you some insider information in return for a lifetime's supply of coffee?'

That made me laugh. 'He already has that. I can't push him; I'll save that for when I'm really struggling.'

I got up to leave and Yeshim muttered another thanks through a mouthful of cookie. At least now I knew that Philippa would have had the opportunity to slip out from the Long Gallery. It was another mark against her.

---

13

*A*s I stepped out into the back lane, a blur of black and white shot round the back of my legs and off towards the garden. It was Romeo, and another larger black-and-white blur was hot on his tail.

'SCOUT, HEEL!'

The Border collie came to a stop with an 'Oh pleeeease, let me play' look on his face.

'Come on, boy.'

Scout slowly walked back towards the muddy Land Rover that was parked outside the security office. His owner, Seth Mellors, the estate gamekeeper, was chewing on a sandwich and chatting to a police officer. Seth and I had exchanged the occasional hello, but he was mainly out and about looking after the 40,000 acres of land – in between being endlessly teased about his surname. Mark for one never called him by his actual name, instead referring to him as Lady Chatterley's lover.

I watched as DS Harnby appeared, escorting a couple of guests out. The day seemed strange and grey, and I felt deflated. I needed to go home, take a long, hot shower and come back tomorrow, ready to start again.

'Hello, Sophie, you look a little more alert.' I had nearly walked into the Duke who was smiling at me, an amused look on his face.

'Afternoon, Duke. I am sorry about this morning.'

'Oh please, don't worry. You gave the Duchess a bit of a laugh when I told her. I take it you've been home.' He glanced at my outfit, but unlike everyone else, he maintained a polite, shock-free expression.

'Oh, no. Joyce had some spare clothing onsite.'

'Ah, that explains it. Do you think we'll be able to open the house to the public tomorrow? The police still seem to be all over it like flies on a corpse.' He paused as he realised what he'd said. 'Oh, I am sorry, that was very inappropriate.' He looked embarrassed, but I waved his comment off. I'd said worse in my time. 'You must have met the victim if he was at the sleepover.'

'I didn't talk to him. He didn't seem too interested in it, the kind of guest who has been dragged there by his wife. But then he was interested in history, so you'd think that he'd be engaged with some of it.'

'And he wasn't?'

'Not really. He didn't seem too happy. In fact, he avoided some of it.' I remembered seeing Thomas outside through the window during the Dickens reading.

The Duke gave a small wave and I turned to see who he was acknowledging. DS Harnby was chatting to someone, but it looked as if she was trying to get away and talk to the Duke.

'Hopefully she'll fill me in, maybe they'll have learnt more about Thomas. Thomas Hattersley, isn't it? You know, I recognise the name. I'm not sure why, but it's ringing bells.' He was staring off down the lane, distracted, presumably trying to work out the connection. 'Ah, she's free. Now go home, I'm sure you're tired.'

I watched as he walked off. Even in jeans and a sweater, he was able to look elegant as he stopped and spoke to DS Harnby. He seemed very calm about the whole affair, the perfect display of the British stiff upper lip. I was keen to follow his instructions, but before I left, I wanted to see Mark. If there was one person who could perk me back up, it was him, plus he'd kill me if I went home without saying goodbye.

Mark shared a big open-plan office with a couple of other tour guides, including Douglas. It was unglamorously located above some of the visitor toilets and overlooked a courtyard, which was eerily quiet for a Sunday afternoon. The door was open. Mark had his feet on his desk and was covering the pages of a book with little pink sticky notes. Douglas was on the far side of the room, reading something on a computer screen, occasionally turning away in order to feed paper into a shredder.

'Can you believe it?' he was complaining. 'She must have written it the minute she got home.'

I remained in the doorway. 'Gentlemen. Working hard?'

Mark didn't move. 'Always,' he responded. I stared at him.

'Don't you stand when a lady enters the room?'

'Refer to my previous answer.' I couldn't help but laugh. He could be so predictable. 'You're letting all the heat out.'

I closed the door behind me, feeling like a nagging mother. I wheeled a chair next to Mark and collapsed into it.

'I've just come to say ta-ra, I'm going home. Caffeine is keeping me standing, but I can feel it swilling round my brain and I'm no use to anyone. I'm done in.'

Douglas let out a loud sigh. 'I wish someone had done *her* in.' He sighed again.

'What are you moaning about?' Mark asked. 'Spit it out instead of huffing and puffing.'

'That sodding woman, she's already written up a review for last night. Trying to get in on the action, I bet, get some publicity for her blog.'

'You mean Philippa?' I asked.

'Who else would take such pleasure in tearing me to shreds in front of the whole world? She's not right in the head, I swear.'

Mark got up and walked over to Douglas, leaning over his shoulder, reading the review.

'Wow, she really doesn't like you.'

'Tell me about it. She's also commented on Lycia's age, not being young enough to play Ellen, and that not all the guests did their research before signing up for the event.'

'That'll be a reference to those who went to the Black Swan,' I commented.

'But then she goes on to talk about Conrad. She reckons he continues to give the, and I quote, "finest portrayal of Charles Dickens in living memory". The rest of the evening gets the thumbs up as well. Of course, she revels in the drama of the night, makes it sound like she was personally at risk and only narrowly escaped the clutches of death. If only.'

He sat back with an air of defeat.

'Wait, she wasn't on your tour, she was on mine. How could she review your tour?'

'She can't, but it doesn't stop her. If you look at it, she's worded it very carefully: "known for his inaccuracies... ever the showman, yet unable to convey the significance of the Fitzwilliam-Scott family's role in British history"...'

Mark glanced up and caught my eye. I saw a very slight smile in the corner of his lips.

'You had that mate of hers. Was he rolling his eyes at every other word?'

'Who?' Douglas had leant forward again and appeared to be re-reading some of the review.

'Thomas, the guy who died. It can be really distracting when he's tutting away, or standing there with a look of disbelief on his face. But you learn to ignore it.'

'Oh him. I didn't notice – I'd never seen him before last night.

She doesn't actually say she was on my tour, but she sure makes it sound like she was.'

'Ignore her.' Mark slapped him on the shoulder in a display of manly support. 'She's just a two-bit blogger with an overblown sense of her own worth.'

'And with 5,000 followers,' Douglas replied dejectedly, feeding more paper into the shredder.

'Why does she hate you so much?' I asked. 'Mark tells me this has been going on for a while. Was she like this when you were working as a tour guide elsewhere?'

'Always. As soon as she found out I'd started doing it, she came along, and the next thing I knew she'd created a blog, and one of the first things on there was a review of my tour. I have wondered if the whole reason she created the site was so she had the chance to get back at me.'

'Why? What did she want to get back at you for?' Philippa was starting to sound a bit obsessive.

'Years ago, we both entered a competition, the Dr Archibald Vogler Award – some old bloke wanted to encourage recent history graduates from Manchester University to pursue careers in the field. You needed to write a history essay. The prize was a couple of hundred quid and your piece went in a national history magazine. We both entered and I won, and she came a close second. That was it, I've had her on my back ever since.'

'I guess you could keep an eye on it and see if she ever gives you reason to pursue her for libel.'

'She's too clever for that.' Douglas turned his computer off with a hard shove of the button. 'I'm done for the day.' He marched out of the room, his frustration clear in every heavy footstep.

'I feel for him,' Mark offered, 'but she's not entirely wrong. He doesn't deserve that, though. I hope enough people have the measure of her. He's still young – well, compared to me – he's got time to improve. Talking of my age, how's my cake coming along? Am I going to have a display of edible artistic magnificence presented to me over dinner, or are you going to poison us all and add to the body count round here?'

'The cake was meant to be a surprise.'

'Look who you're talking to, everything makes it back to me. Every word of gossip or news, every secret can be followed, and at some point it will land on my lap. I'm like a magnet, a walking repository of everything that should be known, everything that shouldn't be known, and everything that is complete and utter rubbish. You baking me a surprise birthday cake was never going to be a surprise, to me or anyone else.'

'Then what flavour is it?' I asked, testing him.

'Carrot cake,' he declared confidently. He was right and laughed at the expression on my face. 'Go home and get some sleep. I'm sure that fat cat of yours is missing you and needs feeding. Although it will probably do her some good to skip a meal or two.'

I playfully flicked the top of his ear as I walked past. Leaving Mark to it, I walked across the courtyard, thinking about a comfy sofa, a soft blanket and a log fire.

Heaven.

The Library Café was empty and the lights off when I returned. Tina had left a note pinned to my office door saying that she'd see me in the morning and to get some sleep. I stuffed my clothes from the previous night into a bag and was about to turn off my computer when curiosity got the better of me.

I typed Douglas's name and 'Dr Archibald Vogler Award' into a search engine and waited. There it was, the 2012 list of winners and runners up, and amongst the names were both Douglas and Philippa. There were also links to their essays. I pulled up Douglas's and started reading. It was about Victorian trade unions; I didn't really know the subject, but it seemed well written.

'You still here?' Joyce had appeared at the door and was looming over me.

'Hmm, I'm just reading through something Douglas wrote years ago.'

'Full of mistakes, I assume? Mark told me he's not exactly a detail man. What is it?'

'Actually it reads pretty well, but I've no idea if it's accurate. It's a competition entry.'

'He cheated,' she said quickly, and with absolute certainty. I laughed.

'You cynic.'

'I mean it. I bet he cheated. His work is always full of mistakes, yet you say it's very well written. Why are you reading that stuff anyway?'

I told her about the review and Philippa's unfair assassination of Douglas's skills.

'Oh dear, sounds like she didn't have a good time. Did she not sleep well?'

'She had a great time. She thinks Conrad was amazing, and the rest of the evening got five stars too. Have a look.' I opened a new window and searched for Philippa's review of the sleepover.

'Oh yes, her darling Conrad. Of course she thought he was fabulous, she's probably still hoping she's in with a chance.'

'She might be now.' I filled Joyce in on Lycia's relationship with Harvey.

'There you go, then.' She was reading the review over my shoulder. 'That's more than a review of Conrad's performance, that's a love letter. He should look out, she doesn't appear to be the full shilling. Does Joe still think that Conrad could have been the actual target?'

'He said they have two lines of enquiry because of the circumstances, yes.'

'Then make sure he has a closer look at that girl. She sounds like she's got a screw loose – who knows what she might do if the man of her dreams has turned her down? And if she isn't aware of Lycia's expeditions into foreign territory, then she might still be mad at him. If she does know about it and thinks he just doesn't want her, then she'll be *really* mad. Either way, he can't win.'

She started buttoning up her jacket.

'I'll see you tomorrow. I presume you're not planning on waking up with the Duke again?' She smirked, and then turned on her heels. 'Goodnight,' she called back over her shoulder as she crossed the café.

I turned off the computer. It was time to finally head home to what was bound to be a very grumpy cat.

14

I threw my dirty clothes on the floor in front of the washing machine and Pumpkin pounced on them. She burrowed her head in amongst the folds of cloth, a habit she has whether the clothes are clean or dirty, but this time she buried hard for a minute or two, and then quickly pulled her head out and turned to face me with a look of fury. She'd smelt Romeo on my clothes – I was in trouble.

Pumpkin is a large, affectionate, very sociable tabby. She has learnt to offer me the top of her head so I can kiss it when I pick her up after arriving home. But she can also perform award-winning sulks, and like most cats, if she isn't in the mood for attention, she lets me know with her claws. I decided that tonight I would steer clear; she could tell me if she wanted stroking. I didn't want to end the day with bloody scratches.

I made sure her food bowl was full and she had clean water, and then I poured myself a drink. I didn't have the energy to craft a decent cocktail; instead, I slugged a double shot of gin into the first glass I could lay my hands on and threw some tonic on top. Not too much; tonight my gin did not need watering down. I took it with me to the bedroom and put on my pyjamas; this glass wasn't leaving my hand, even for a minute.

Next it was back downstairs to the fire. I had become pretty adept at getting my log fire going and it wasn't long until it was roaring away and I was sprawled out on the sofa, a furry blanket over my legs. Pumpkin had taken up position within a whisker's length of the fire and was cleaning herself.

I closed my eyes. I wanted to be able to put some clear thought into the events of the last twenty-four hours, but all I ended up with was a dead man who had no apparent connection with the house and fifty-nine other guests about whom I knew nothing. I started to drift off. The heat of the fire was sinking into my bones and the sound of the wood crackling gave me something to focus on, other than the image of a dead Charles Dickens that kept popping into my mind.

Ooomph! There was a sudden weight on my chest and the air shot out of me. My eyes popped open and I was nose to nose with Pumpkin. She sniffed my face, gave my chin a quick lick, and then settled down, staring at me. I wasn't sure if I was forgiven or if this was her unsubtle way of saying, 'I'm watching you.' There was something comforting about the weight of her on my chest and I closed my eyes again, only to rapidly open them as my phone rang.

I stretched my arm out and fumbled around on the floor. I couldn't find it.

'I'm sorry, Pumpkin, I'm going to have to...' She leapt off as I rolled over further than she was comfortable with. Finally, my fingers met my phone.

'Hello?'

'Were you asleep?' It was Mark.

'Not yet, I was having quality time with Pumpkin.'

'She's forgiven your betrayal?'

'Well I wouldn't go that far, but she hasn't drawn blood yet. What do you want?'

'Oh, very nice, "What do you want?" On the eve of my birthday, I'd expect a little more warmth.'

'Stop milking it, you only get special treatment on the day itself. So, my dear, how may I help your good self? Is that better?'

I heard him give a little harrumph. 'I thought you might like to know that DS Harnby came to see me after you left.'

I dragged myself upright. 'Go on.'

'They found a manuscript amongst Thomas's things and the content seems to relate to Charleton House. They needed someone to have a read through it and see if anything stands out.'

'Does it?'

'I don't know, I've only had it an hour. I'm going to head home and make a start on it. I'll let you know what I think as soon as I'm done, just thought you'd want to know as I'm sure the race is on to solve the case before the police.'

'It's never been that.' I was a little hurt. He made it sound like I had something to prove, some sort of vendetta against them. Joe was my friend, I just kept getting caught up in these things.

Mark must have picked up on my feelings. 'I'm only kidding. You need to get some sleep, girl, you're getting sensitive.' He was right. I'm never at my best when I'm tired. 'I'll come by the café in the morning and tell you all about it while you stick a birthday candle in a chocolate croissant. Goodnight.'

He hung up and I swapped the phone for what remained of the gin and tonic. With my glass drained, I lay back down. Mark would be in his element, under police orders to read a book about Charleton House. It was the perfect birthday present.

I had no idea how long I'd been asleep when my phone rang again, but the fire was down to embers and needed another log. Pumpkin was asleep at my feet and I was groggy. I looked at the screen on my phone: 'Joe Greene'.

'Hey, Joe,' I slurred. 'Hang on.' I got up slowly, trying not to disturb Pumpkin, and threw another log on the fire. 'Okay, I'm back.'

'I hope it's not too late to be calling?'

'I have no idea what time it is, so I'll let you be the judge of that.' Trying to keep my tone light, I wandered through to the kitchen. 'So, have you cracked it?' I asked. 'Is the killer at the station now, sobbing out a confession?' I grabbed a block of cheese out of the fridge; I was hungry and fancied a toastie. Quick and easy, that was the kind of food I needed tonight.

'Ha, I wish. No, I wanted to run something by you. Did you know about the drinks party that Conrad and the others were at after the sleepover?'

'I wouldn't call it a party, but some of them stayed for a drink. I heard about it from Betsy, and then Conrad mentioned it to me, and that there was a disagreement. I had no idea it was happening. I'd probably fallen asleep in the library by then.'

He laughed. 'You give new meaning to "the body was found in the library".' I noticed that he didn't comment on my chat with Conrad. Normally he'd tell me off for sticking my nose in. Maybe he was getting used to it, maybe he realised it was a lost cause. It was hardly my fault if people found me easy to open up to, or at least that was my excuse.

'Okay, I'm just wondering where Lycia and Harvey went after the arguments started, but there are a few discrepancies about the timing of things. They could have gone straight home, or they might have been hanging around the house another hour or so before they left, depending on who you talk to. Everyone seems a bit cagey, and security don't have a full record of people coming and going. We'll get the thumbscrews out in the morning and try and pin the timeline down.'

'You think that Lycia or Harvey might have stayed onsite long enough to kill Thomas, thinking it was Conrad?'

'I'm just trying to be sure of people's movements, but we're not ruling out their developing relationship as a possible motive.'

'While we're talking about relationships, what about Philippa?' I asked.

'What about her? She's reached your list of suspects?'

'Well she's part of that whole love triangle thing, and Joyce made a comment this afternoon that got me thinking.'

Joe laughed. 'Joyce? Don't tell me she's taken on the role of detective as well?'

'Oh God, no, can you imagine? She has the subtlety of a sledgehammer. Mind you, she could terrify people into confessing with a single glance. No, she made a comment about Philippa still being in love with Conrad. He reckons it's all calmed down and everything is fine, but Joyce thinks she's still harbouring a passion for him.' I told him about the review, and about Philippa's reason for resenting Douglas. 'She seems able to fixate in a really unhealthy way. She's still taking her anger out on Douglas, in public, seven years after the competition. That's not exactly the action of someone who is of sane mind.'

Joe was quiet, then he said something I never thought I'd hear.

'You know, Joyce might be onto something. Obsessive, capable of holding on to a grudge, pent up anger. I'll call Harnby, discuss it with her.'

'It's a bit late, isn't it? What time is it?' I looked at my phone. It was nine o'clock, not as late as I'd thought.

'No, she'll still be at the office. I think DI Flynn is starting to put her under pressure, and anyway, I don't think she knows how to relax. Thanks, Soph.'

'Come on, anything else you can let me in on before you go?'

'You don't give up, do you. No, nothing new, although we did get the pathologist's report back. It seems that Thomas was punched before he was stabbed.'

'So there was a fight?'

'I wouldn't go as far as that, a bit of a scuffle maybe, and then what looks like a punch to the side of his face. It wouldn't have contributed to his death.' He paused. 'You know, I remember when we would talk about things other than murder. One of these days, we should have a drink, but rule that subject strictly off limits.'

He was right, it did seem to be one of our few topics of conversation.

'That would be lovely. We can make a start tomorrow night.'

'What's tomorrow?'

'Mark's birthday. You know he'll want to be the centre of attention all day, and probably for the rest of the week.'

'Oh hell, it had completely slipped my mind. I don't even have a card. He'll kill me, and I can't just go to an all-night petrol station and get a dreadful card and some battered flowers.'

'Luckily for you, I have a drawer full of cards. I'll bring one in for you. Just make sure you find me before you run into him. You can tell him his present is on the way but the delivery is late and it will help him stretch the fun throughout the week.'

'Sophie, you're a star. I owe you big time.'

'Yep, this is more urgent than solving the murder.'

After we'd hung up, I broke up the fire, and then set off up the stairs to bed, dragging the blanket behind me like a tired child, a cheese toastie in the other hand. I was done, the cogs were about to stop turning. I had to sleep in a proper bed, even if it did quickly become a crumb-filled one. I needed the energy to cope with the royal birthday in the morning – lots of energy.

15

I was fully prepared for the moment that Mark burst dramatically through the Library Café doors. It wouldn't have been right for me to cover the café in banners and streamers, particularly as I'd been told we could reopen to the public today, but I had prepared a table for him. A 'Happy Birthday' napkin and paper plate awaited him, along with a tall pointy gold cardboard hat. His birthday card was on the plate, but he'd have to wait until the evening for his edible present.

'I see no expense has been spared,' was his sarcastic greeting. He grinned and kissed me on the cheek. 'I love it, thank you.'

'Take a seat, Your Majesty, I'll be back in a minute.'

I returned from the kitchen with a chocolate croissant, his favourite, a single candle stuck in the top. I carried it slowly, not wanting to blow out the flame. Behind me, Tina carried his mug of coffee, and together we sang a rather disturbing rendition of 'Happy Birthday'.

Mark glanced around the room. 'No, no windows were shattered. Thank you both,' he said when we'd finished.

'I hope the candle sets your 'tache on fire,' Tina called over her shoulder as she returned to the kitchen. Mark took an enormous bite of the croissant, leaving a collection of flaky pastry crumbs along his moustache, which had survived the blowing out of the candle fully intact. He grinned at me.

'Thank you,' he mumbled. I passed him his card. He ripped it open and laughed at the picture of a muscular naked young man who was holding a strategically placed birthday cake.

'I hope *he's* coming tonight.'

'So, has Bill been pampering you all morning?'

'Not a chance. He had a staff meeting first thing this morning and he's giving a presentation. Something to do with the latest round of testing the poor kids are going to be subjected to.'

Bill was a history teacher at a local secondary school. I knew he loved working with the children, even the distracted teenagers, but disliked the amount of paperwork that was being added to a teacher's workload and showed no sign of letting up.

'But he did bring me coffee in bed before he flew out of the door, and when I went downstairs there was the most enormous bouquet of flowers on the dining table.'

'That'll be a yes, then,' I said. 'You're a lucky man.'

A gentle smile appeared on his lips and he nodded.

'I'm a *very* lucky man.' He pulled out his phone. 'Look at these, aren't they beautiful?' He showed me a photo of the most enormous bouquet of roses and carnations. I could see in the background that Bill had also hung up a 'Happy Birthday' banner.

'So lucky that I'll get you a second coffee before your first runs out.'

I went back up to the counter just as Tina walked out of the kitchen.

She leant over and whispered, 'There's a strange man at the window, I think he wants you.'

I left her to make Mark's coffee and went into the kitchen, wondering what I was going to be dragged into next. I needn't have worried. I was greeted by Joe Greene's face peering through the glass.

'Sophie...' I couldn't make out the rest so I opened the window 'Do you have the card for Mark? I know he's in there with you.'

I laughed and fetched it from my office. 'I hope this'll do.' The card joked about Mark looking great for his age, if you squinted.

'Perfect, I don't want him getting complacent. Have you got a...' Before he could finish, I handed him a pen. 'Thanks, be there in a minute.'

I returned to the café to find Tina and Mark admiring the young man on his card. They were still discussing it when Joe walked in and stuck his head between theirs.

'Not bad. You'd only need a cupcake though, eh, Mark? Here you are, happy birthday.' Joe handed him the card and slapped him on the shoulder.

'Bill mentioned he came with baggage,' said Mark. 'It's only recently that I've realised he meant you.' He read the card and raised his eyebrows at his brother-in-law. 'Cheeky sod! Thanks, Joe.' His smile was genuine. 'You still coming tonight?'

'I hope so, assuming we make some kind of progress on the case.'

Mark glanced up at me. 'It looks like you might be first past the post, Mistress Poirot.'

I was pleased that Joe decided to ignore the comment.

'Now I've done my brotherly duty, I need to go and get some work done. I'm meeting Harnby.'

Tina placed a takeout cup of coffee in front of Joe. 'I'm sure you'll be needing this. Do you want me to make one you can take to your boss, start the day on the right side of her?'

Joe grinned. 'Yes please, Tina. How did you know I wouldn't be staying?'

'Because you're not stupid enough to be lounging around here while your boss is trying to solve a murder. A takeout cup shows you've not settled in for a chat, but you're ready to spring into action at a moment's notice. I'll be back in a minute.'

Joe watched her walk off. He looked a bit sheepish.

'To be honest, I never thought of that. Maybe I should always have my coffee in a takeout cup. It'll make me look more dynamic.'

'Absolutely,' confirmed Mark with a little too much assurance. 'It can be your new superhero symbol. Rip off that spectacularly pedestrian-looking shirt and underneath is a Lycra vest with a picture of a takeout coffee cup on it. The stronger the roast, the more crimes you solve. Captain Coffee to the rescue.'

He mimed a salute. Joe shook his head.

'If it wasn't your birthday…'

Tina arrived just in time to interrupt.

'Two coffees, and one detective sergeant walking down the lane. You should get your skates on, Captain Coffee.'

Joe raised his eyebrows at his new nickname, but smiled at Tina.

'Cheers. Well, I guess Captain Coffee better go save the day. See you motley lot later.'

I turned back to Mark as Joe left. He was staring intently at me.

'I'm getting old.'

'What?'

He looked down at the card of the muscular young man. 'It's finally happening, I'm getting old.'

'You're two years younger than me!' I exclaimed.

'And you're almost entirely grey. Is that what I've got to look forward to?'

'Yes, and you're going to shrink a foot too.'

'Do you think Bill will want a younger model?'

'He already has one, you're ten years younger than him.'

'Precisely. He met me when I was *much* younger, so maybe I'm getting too old for him. Maybe he prefers men under forty.'

'Then you've got three years to convince him to hang on to

you. Anyway, I wouldn't worry. Mentally and emotionally, you're barely out of your teens.'

He stuck his tongue out at me. He needed distracting.

'So, what did you discover?'

'Where?'

'The book. The manuscript that Harnby asked you to read. Have you finished it? Was there anything useful?'

He took a deep breath and appeared to refocus himself.

'Almost. I have no idea if it will help the case, but it makes for a decent read. There's some general history, and then it focuses largely on the Fitzwilliam-Scott family's role in British politics. A rehashing of some old arguments about their significance, but it comes firmly down on their side.'

'Do you think Thomas wrote it?'

Mark had pulled the manuscript out of his bag and was idly flicking through the pages as he spoke.

'Possibly. Bill said that he was very keen on history and wiped the floor with the other teams at the pub quiz. I would guess he's local, so he'd be familiar with the house and the family. It would make sense for it to be a subject he wanted to write about. I'd need to see something else he's written to check it's the same style to be certain, but I don't see why not.'

'Do you think this was why he was killed?'

'The book? No idea.'

I drank the cold dregs of my coffee and thought about Thomas. We knew next to nothing about him, except that he might not actually have been the intended victim. When I looked up, it was nine o'clock and staff were starting to trickle in, wanting to get a coffee and pastry to take back to their desks. Although today I knew they would linger and chat with their colleagues, hoping to get some gossip about the events of the weekend. Tina and Chelsea seemed to be coping fine and I was desperate to start digging around for more information. I was feeling like a caged animal; it was time to escape for a little while.

'Come on, birthday boy, you must have work to do.'

Mark pushed his chair back and started to gather his things.

'I need to finish the book before Harnby gets back if nothing else, then I've promised to write an article for a local newspaper, "Life as a Tour Guide" sort of thing. I figure that will be enough – I don't want to overexert myself on such a historic day.'

'Historic?' I queried, and then realised. 'Oh, your birthday. Yes, one for the history books.'

16

*A*fter tidying up the evidence of our little birthday breakfast, I had a quiet word with Tina, grabbed a couple of bags of Charleton House chocolates and a jar of honey, and jumped in my car. Normally I'd enjoy the scenery as I drove, relishing the sweep of the narrow country roads and the rolling hills beyond the dry stone walls. I'd play my music loud and, if it wasn't too cold, wind the windows down and enjoy a blast of fresh air.

This time, however, I was on a mission. I wanted to know more about Douglas and his relationship with Philippa; I figured it might tell me about Philippa's state of mind. Finding out more about her relationship with Conrad was also on my to-do list. I ignored the claustrophobic fog that had crept over the fields and shot around the bends much faster than was safe, heading to one of my favourite Derbyshire villages. Tina lived in Hathersage, about twenty minutes' drive away, and so did Philippa. With a concerned but resigned look on her face, Tina had told me exactly where Philippa was to be found.

. . .

Hathersage is a picturesque village that would be overrun with visitors in the warmer weather. St Michael and All Angels' church is famous for being the reputed burial site of Little John, Robin Hood's sidekick. Philippa lived a few hundred yards away from the church in a small stone cottage. As I stood outside, I recognised Tina's house further down the lane from photos she'd shown me of her garden.

I grabbed the chocolates off the passenger seat, took a deep breath and walked up the path to the front door. Philippa opened the door before I'd finished knocking and peered at me with a quizzical expression on her face. She looked rather ordinary now she was out of her straw yellow dress, an oversized t-shirt hanging over tight-fitting jeans, her impressive, curvy figure not quite as eye-catching. I could only assume that Conrad had fallen for the persona she created at events.

'Oh hello, you're... weren't you at the sleepover?'

'Yes, I work at the house. I'm Sophie, Head of Catering.'

'Do you often make house calls?'

'No, no, I'm just... here.' I thrust the bags of chocolate at her. 'We wanted to check that our guests were okay – the local ones, anyway – and we hope you'll come back again soon.' I was rambling and talking rubbish, but I wanted to get in the front door. 'How are you?'

'Fine.' She still looked rather confused. 'I guess I should invite you in.'

'Thank you.' I brushed past her before she had a chance to change her mind. 'Should I go in here?' I walked through an open door and into a sitting room with a rather old and tired-looking moss-green sofa. The rug on the floor had seen a lot of use and was bare in patches. She took a seat in a matching green armchair and indicated that I should sit on the sofa.

'How are things at the house?' Philippa asked. 'Are the police still there?'

'They are. We're open to the public again, but they're still finishing off. I'm sorry about your friend. Were you close?'

She laughed, and then started coughing. 'Thomas? Oh God, no. I'm friends with his wife, but Thomas and I have never exactly seen eye to eye. Still, it is shocking.'

'You must be so relieved it wasn't Conrad.'

'Conrad? Why would I have thought it was Conrad?' She looked at me blankly.

'You didn't know? It was initially thought that the victim was Conrad, they were dressed very similarly.'

She let out a puff of air and slumped back in her chair. 'I had no idea. I'm glad I didn't realise at the time.'

'You and Conrad are close?'

She sat up and eyed me suspiciously. 'I'm guessing you know the answer to that question. I know how quickly gossip spreads around that place, so why don't you tell me why you're really here? And don't tell me it's to deliver chocolates.'

I stared at my hands for a moment, wondering how to approach the subject. We'd got to the point quicker than I'd intended.

'You're right, I know about what happened. Conrad says you've remained on good terms.'

'As much as we can under the circumstances. We don't talk anymore, it's better that way.'

'What about Lycia?'

'What about her? I'm sure she hates my guts. I'm not proud of what we did, of what I did. We just got caught up in the moment.' She was playing with the hem of her t-shirt, a thread gradually getting longer and longer as she wrapped it round the end of her finger.

'How did you feel when they got back together?'

'How did I feel? Do you mean was I wracked with jealousy? Had I been imaging a perfect life with Conrad? Two-point-four children, growing old together? I had a moment of envy, yes, but it *was* momentary, and I always knew nothing would come of our... our... well, I moved on. I had to. I knew Lycia had put rules in place for Conrad and I did what I could to make it easy for him to follow them. But I didn't stay away entirely. I wasn't going to stop attending events. I still have my blog to write, and anyway, I wasn't the only guilty party.'

She sounded so reasonable, almost too reasonable. There was a sadness woven between the words as she spoke, but I didn't detect any bitterness. It was time to change the subject.

'There's something else I wanted to ask you. Can you tell me anything about Douglas Popplewell? I know you knew him years ago, and I know you don't get on. What happened?'

She visibly relaxed as I steered the conversation in this new direction.

'Douglas? Do you think he might be involved?'

I shrugged. 'I don't know for sure, I'm just curious about a couple of things.'

'Douglas is a cheat, or at least he was, and my guess is he still is. You look surprised by my bluntness, but it's the truth.'

'Tell me.'

'He cheated in a competition we entered just after we graduated from university.'

'The Dr Archibald Vogler Award?'

'You've heard of it? It can kick-start people's careers. At the time it was considered really important for students who wanted to get research funding. Douglas entered an essay written by someone else and won.'

'You know this for sure?'

'I can't prove it, but yes, I'm sure. A group of students were found guilty of plagiarism around that time. There was a bit of a racket going on, students were writing essays for cash, and Douglas was friends with a couple of them. His name came up in gossip at the time, but he was never pulled into the investigation formally – as far as I know, anyway. His grades were okay, not great, but the essay he submitted for the competition was *really* good. Too good for it to be his work. But I couldn't prove it, so they dismissed my concerns and he won.' She sounded both angry and resigned to it.

'But why keep on attacking him in your blog? It was so long ago.'

'I only write what I see.'

'Maybe, but you're pretty harsh in the way you do it.'

'Perhaps. He deserves it, though. He's probably spent his whole career to date riding on other people's coat tails. I'm just trying to ground him.'

'Very publicly.'

'Is there anything else you wanted to ask me? Only I have work to do.'

I'd tested her patience to its limits. I shook my head.

'No. Actually, I'm sorry to ask, but could I use your bathroom? I don't think I'll make it back to the house.' I'd had four mugs of coffee since I'd got out of bed and I was regretting at least one of them.

'It's up the stairs on the left. You can see yourself out.'

The stairs were steep and narrow, and I was grateful for the light that was suddenly flicked on for me. Before I turned into the bathroom, I peered into the room opposite. A large antique wooden bed dominated the room – it must have been hell to get it up the stairs. At the foot of it, a heavy wooden chest of drawers held a number of photos.

I stepped closer; they were all photos of Charles Dickens. Well, I say all, but some were postcard reproductions of paintings, and all of them were of Conrad. Joyce hadn't been wrong. Despite everything Philippa had just told me, it looked as if she hadn't let go of Conrad yet.

Beside the photos were multiple copies of Dickens's books, a dried red geranium, and a little figurine of Dickens. On the wall above were posters of Dickens's book covers and a framed collection of tickets from staged versions of his work she must have attended over the years. An article about Conrad and a reading he had given in London last month had been printed from the internet and lay next to the books.

I heard footsteps downstairs and dashed out of the room. Going into the bathroom to flush the toilet, I then ran down the stairs.

'Thank you, bye,' I called as I left. I was going to have to drive back with my legs crossed.

17

*A*fter running from my car, elbowing my way past a few visitors and making it to the car park toilets just in time, I walked back down the lane, thinking about the shrine to Conrad that Philippa had in her bedroom. I was wondering how much of what she'd said I could believe when I spotted the Duke, who waved at me.

'Hold up, Sophie, I've remembered why Thomas Hattersley's name rang bells. We used to have a team of locals who would come and work as beaters during the pheasant shoots. They'd flush the birds out from the undergrowth for the hunting party. Arnold Hattersley was one of the regulars and he'd sometimes get extra work with the gamekeeper throughout the rest of the year. But he got caught up with some sort of poaching.'

'When was this?' I asked.

'I had a quick look back over some of our annual reports. Early nineties. I think it all came to light in 1992, but the poaching had been going on for a while.'

'And how is Thomas linked to all this?'

'Arnold was his dad and a young Thomas used to come to work with him from time to time. I asked the Duchess about it and she remembered a rather chubby, spotty teenager. He must have been about eighteen. I don't remember a lot more about it, but the current gamekeeper might have some files in his office. I hope this is of some use?'

'Yes, absolutely. Thank you.' My heart was starting to race; this was the first bit of really useful information I had, although it opened up the field of people who might have known Thomas. Maybe he had been the intended target after all.

Seth Mellors had been the gamekeeper for less than a year; he'd started not all that long after me and I knew him by name and sight only. He was always in a green wax jacket and a flat cap, his Border collie by his side. He'd park his muddy Land Rover on the back lane and spend time with the security team; their jobs often crossed over and they helped each other out, but I'd had no reason to be in meetings with him. For all I knew, he wasn't a coffee drinker, unless he made his own. I'd never seen him in any of the cafés.

His office was just off the yard that was home to the gardens team. He had a small room in a single-storey stone building, his desk was in front of the window, and I could see him working on his computer as I approached. He looked up and I gave a little wave, pointing at his door questioningly. He stood up and opened it.

'Hi, do you have a few minutes?' He stepped back to let me in and Scout quickly got up to take a sniff of me.

'Scout, back to your bed. Course. I've seen you around, but I don't know your name.'

'Sophie, I run the cafés. Here, it's a chocolate brownie.'

'Thanks. Is this in case I don't believe you?' He smiled and ripped the bag open, making a start on its contents before he'd even sat back down. 'Pull up a seat. I'm just working on some reports, but I'm happy to take a break. How can I help?'

'I'm trying to find out about an incident a few decades back, around 1992. I was hoping you'd have some record of it in your files.'

I turned to look at the row of shelves on the back wall, packed with battered folders and boxes, surprised at how plain the room was. I'm not sure what I was expecting. Guns leaning in the corner, maybe; perhaps a couple of rabbits hanging off the back of the door. But this was just a regular office. A tall locked cabinet was in one corner, Scout making himself comfortable next to it, and a couple of pairs of muddy boots were in another. An enormous map of the entire estate took up one wall. A small fridge was next to Seth's desk with a kettle and jar of instant coffee on top.

'What sort of incident?' he asked.

'Poaching.'

'Well, there's been a bit of that over the years. You might have to help me narrow it down.'

'It was one of the staff, a beater by the name of Arnold Hattersley.'

Seth stood up and reached for a file. 'I know exactly what you mean. I've been going through all this lot, trying to tidy things up, plus plenty of people have been happy to tell the new boy all the gossip. Especially when it relates to previous people in this job.'

He sat back down with a tired-looking brown file.

'This should really be with Human Resources cos it relates to an ex-employee. It shouldn't just be sat on my shelves. I'll get round to it eventually.' He flicked through the papers until he found what he was looking for. 'Bernie Stubbs was in my job then. He was the gamekeeper from 1962. In 1990, after a couple of quiet years, poaching started up again. Just bits here and there, but regular. No one could figure it out. Eventually someone pointed the finger at Bernie. It was always on his days off and holidays, or when his own small team was involved in a big project and not doing their day-to-day work. On those days, security were also short-staffed or preoccupied. All that required inside knowledge, and for some reason the powers that be decided it was Bernie. He denied all knowledge, but was suspended anyway.

'Turned out it was actually the work of Arnold Hattersley, a beater. He knew most of the team, game keeping and security. He'd drink with them down the pub so he knew all the goings on, and used that information to work out when the best time was to come and set traps. I don't know how they caught him, but he was arrested and eventually pleaded guilty. Bernie came back to work, but in 1993 he retired. Died a couple of years later. Is that what you're looking for?'

'That's exactly it. Is there anything in there about a Thomas Hattersley?'

Seth took a few minutes to go through the file.

'No, nothing. Who was he?'

'He was Arnold's son.'

'The dead guy from the other night?' He sounded surprised. 'It really is a small world.'

'I was wondering who might know Thomas from back when this all kicked off with his dad.'

'Well, the gamekeeper that took over from Bernie in '93 left in 2002. His successor left last year, and that's when I came along. So there's been a few of us since then.'

'What about family? Wasn't there a lot of jobs for the family in those days?'

Seth nodded. 'Yeah, key way to get jobs then, but as far as I know, Bernie didn't have any kids of his own. The two game-keepers that followed on were father and son, so in that case, yes. But they weren't related to Bernie, they were a new lot.'

'And you?' I decided to risk the question for no reason other than curiosity. 'Are you related to anyone here?'

He laughed. 'No, my dad's a plumber. The closest my family

ever got to the great outdoors was sticking a bird feeder in the back garden.'

'So how did you end up doing this?'

'School. I had an amazing geography teacher who was a volunteer park ranger in the holidays and also loved to clay pigeon shoot. Took me under his wing. And with a name like mine, what else was I going to do?' He grinned. 'Is there anything else I can help you with?'

'No, that's great. Thanks, Seth.' I looked at the jar of instant coffee. 'And pop round the café anytime you want a decent cup of coffee, it's on the house.'

'If you chuck in another brownie, you'll see me before the week is out.' He winked and I let myself out of the door.

So Thomas had had a connection to the house, but he hadn't been the one poaching, as far as the records showed. I did the maths – as the Duke had said, he would have been about eighteen when his dad was caught, so old enough to be involved. Still, it could just be a coincidence that he was here when he was killed. He was a local man born and bred and he loved history. There were plenty of people who lived in the surrounding villages with connections to Charleton House, he was in no way unique. He was, however, the only one of them who had been murdered here.

I left behind the warmth of Seth's office and nearly fell over Romeo. He was patrolling the yard – this was very much his home turf – and he paid no attention to me.

'Romeo, here.' I clicked my fingers and crouched down. I couldn't resist a cute cat or dog – make that anything with fur. Romeo stopped, looked back over his shoulder at me, made an assessment that didn't go in my favour and carried on his way.

I wasn't giving up that easily, so I followed him towards the tall stone wall that ran the length of the yard. Finally he turned and allowed me to pet him. I picked him up. He was feather light compared to Pumpkin, who was going to put my back out one of these days.

'Why did you say it if you didn't mean it?' The man's voice sounded desperate and angry. I looked around; I couldn't see anyone in the yard.

'I'm sorry.' Now it was a woman speaking. The voice was familiar – both were.

'I thought you wanted to leave him.'

'I did, maybe… I don't know, but he's tried so hard. And when I thought he was dead…'

'You realised you couldn't live without him, is that it? I can't believe this! You've made a fool of me.'

I could hear the man start to walk away, then stop and return.

'There isn't anything I wouldn't do for you.'

It sounded like a row between Harvey and Lycia, but I needed to be sure. I looked around. There was a heavy-duty golf cart parked further along the wall with a flat bed at the back so the gardeners could carry equipment round the house gardens. It would be easy to stand on.

I put Romeo down, took a handful of skirt and pulled myself up onto the flat bed. From there, I had a clear view of the walled garden, and sticking my head over a bit further, I confirmed the source of the voices.

Harvey was pacing up and down.

'I've been a bloody idiot.' He punched the wall and I winced – that had to hurt. 'I told you I'd do anything, and I still would. He doesn't deserve you. This all would have been so much easier if it was him who'd been killed.'

'Oh my God, Harvey, you can't mean that…' Lycia looked horror-stricken.

'Can I help?' The voice came from behind me. 'You can get into the garden through a gate, climbing the wall isn't necessary.'

Seth was standing next to the cart, looking bemused and offering me his hand. I wanted to stay, hear a confession from

Harvey – if that was where the conversation was going – but I guessed I'd have missed it by now.

I took Seth's hand. 'I was just checking to see where... where Romeo had gone.' That was the best I could do at short notice.

'Romeo is fine. In fact, if you ask him nicely, I reckon he'll drive you back to your office.'

He nodded towards the driver's seat of the golf cart. Romeo was sitting facing the steering wheel, looking for all the world like he was about to turn the key and start the engine.

'Thanks, but I think I'll walk.'

Seth nodded, looking like he was stifling a laugh. I couldn't blame him. As soon as I was out of earshot, I burst out laughing myself. I must have looked like such a fool.

But I soon stopped laughing when Harvey strode past me, his face full of fury. Conrad hadn't been convinced that Harvey was capable of murder, but maybe he'd been wrong.

18

I was still smiling to myself about Seth finding me perched on top of a golf cart when Betsy ran past, dressed in full servants' garb. She waved at me.

'Betsy,' I called after her. 'Do you have a minute?'

'Hang on, I need to get this to an education group in the courtyard. Come with me.' She was carrying a hessian sack in one hand and her long skirt in the other. It looked a little like the outfits Tina and Chelsea had worn on the night of the sleepover when they were serving dinner. In fact, she was probably wearing some of the exact same items. I had no idea what live interpretation piece she was working on today, but she was clearly a 19th century servant.

I followed on behind, ducked through a low doorway, down a narrow whitewashed corridor and into a courtyard full of schoolchildren.

'Betsy, thank God.' A young woman grabbed the sack from her and dashed back to the group of children before bellowing, 'Follow me, everyone, we'll head to the classrooms.'

'You wanted me?' Betsy turned to face me. 'I've a few minutes before the next group turns up, let's sit over there.' She led me to a bench in a far corner and pulled a shawl around her as we sat down. She didn't look dressed for the weather; I just hoped she had plenty of thermals on under her costume.

'I wanted to ask you about Conrad and Philippa. Just how unpleasant did all that get?'

'Pretty bad. Lycia blew her top a couple of times. Most of the time, everyone was very professional – in public, at least.'

'Was Philippa... well, did she keep pursuing it?'

'Do you mean was she some kind of crazed stalker who would do anything for Conrad, and when she didn't get him, she killed him? Or someone she thought was him.'

I smiled sheepishly; I wasn't being very subtle.

'I actually started to feel sorry for her. She's brash and doesn't have complete control of her volume dial sometimes, but I don't think she's as bad as people say. I get the impression the whole thing just got out of control. She was devastated when things got so nasty between Conrad and Lycia, and I think she regrets it all as much as he does. She became the fall guy.'

It made a change to talk to someone who sounded like they actually had some sympathy for Philippa.

'What do you mean?'

'I know that Conrad had wanted to handle it all a bit more carefully, tell Lycia himself. He knew what he'd done was wrong, but he at least had the decency to want to take responsibility.'

'And he didn't?'

'Didn't have the chance. Someone beat him to it. Whoever it was found out, and then broke the news to Lycia.'

The peace of the courtyard was broken as another school group flooded in, screaming and running, a teacher struggling to get them to pay any attention to her.

'I need to go, introduce that lot to the world *below stairs*.'

'Wait, do you know who told Lycia?'

'No, but it happened after an event at Berwick Hall, that much I remember. We were all getting ready to go and I saw Lycia reading a note. The next minute, she was driving out of the car park so fast, I thought she was going to kill someone. It all came out the next day. I have to go, sorry.'

I watched as Betsy effortlessly took charge of the group, leaving the teacher to resemble a spare part. It wouldn't be long until the teachers abandoned their charges and found their way to a café. Completely against the rules, but it hadn't stopped them before.

I warmed myself up by assisting behind the counter and giving Tina a break. Staff that came in were continuing to gossip, and it hadn't taken long for people to find out that I was the one who had found Thomas, although the stories varied as to whether he had been stabbed with Charles Dickens's quill or beaten with a copy of *A Christmas Carol*.

Once Tina returned, I decided to distract myself with Mark's cake. I wasn't a professional baker, just a keen amateur, but my interest and reasonable skill level meant I occasionally helped out and made cookies and cakes for the cafés, taking the pressure off our part-time pastry chef.

I was standing in front of three rectangular carrot cakes that I was about to decorate to look like books – I must have been drunk when I'd offered to make Mark's birthday cake. I'd planned on making a pile of five books, but I quickly realised that was overambitious and cut it down to four. Then I'd dropped one cake while taking it out of the oven, so four became three. Right now, they looked less like books and more like squashed bricks lying side by side. It was time to place them in a pile.

I carefully slid a large knife under one and ever so slowly brought it over the largest of the three. I wanted the books to look a little untidy, like Mark's desk, so I turned it slightly and lowered it. Perfect. Now for the third. I repeated the process and held it over the other two, trying to decide which way to lay it. Did I want the books in a sort of spiral, or...

There was a knock at the window. I looked up. At the same time I could feel the knife tilt. I looked back in time to see the third and final cake drop off the knife, slide down the side of the other two, and then fall off the counter into a pile on my foot.

'NOOOOOOO! DAG NAMMIT, NOT AGAIN. WHAT?'

Joe stood in the window, looking very sheepish. 'Sorry,' he mouthed. I jabbed my thumb in the air, firmly indicating that he should come in.

'Bloody idiot,' I muttered to no one in particular, scooping up the cake off the floor. I was dumping the last handful in the bin as a white paper napkin was stuck round the door and waved in the air.

'Is it safe?' Joe's voice drifted through.

'You muppet!' I exclaimed, this time loud enough for him to hear. 'I'm coming.'

Joe turned down the offer of a coffee, but I felt the need to start mainlining the stuff again. Something had to get me through the next stage of decorating the cake, what was left of it.

'I'll buy you a new pair.' Joe was looking at my shoes, one of which was now smeared in cream and crumbs. I'd wiped off the worst of it, but it was still a mess.

'Okay, but they're very expensive designer trainers that you can only purchase in person in New York.' I grinned. 'Don't be soft; you'll do no such thing. Right, seeing as you're here...'

I proceeded to tell him about the conversation I'd overheard between Harvey and Lycia, missing out the embarrassing bit about Seth and Romeo's cameo. I decided to save the information about the note to Lycia until I knew more.

Joe took a deep breath. 'Our list of suspects isn't getting any shorter.'

'And I'm about to make it longer.' He tilted his head and waited. 'I have a confession to make. Please don't get mad – you know what I'm like and I'm only trying to help.'

'What have you done? Have you been wearing that damned deerstalker hat again?'

'What?'

'Have you been playing detective? I've told you before, leave this to the professionals. So what have you done?'

I told him about my visit to see Philippa and watched the storm clouds gather across his face as I spoke.

'Sophie, I can't believe you did that. Harnby will hit the roof.'

'Does she have to know?'

'She'll probably find out, especially as Philippa now seems to deserve a visit from us. You're bound to come up in conversation.'

'But if I hadn't gone, you wouldn't know to pay her a visit.'

'Don't you dare try to dig yourself out of this one, Sophie Lockwood.'

We sat in silence for a few minutes, until I decided to break it.

'Do you have any idea why Thomas had the manuscript on him? Presumably it was his own work.'

Joe sighed and shook his head.

'Not necessarily. He was a history teacher, but did a bit of editing work on the side. His wife said that he wasn't really qualified, but he'd help people out by reading through their work and giving feedback for a small fee. It helped subsidise his teacher's salary, and she'd been out of work for a while, so the money was helpful.'

'If he's a history teacher, doesn't Bill know him from school as well as the quiz?'

'I already checked, no. Thomas taught at a school on the far side of Sheffield, and he wasn't much of a talker at those quiz nights, so Bill never knew much about him.' He glanced at his watch. 'I should be off.'

'It's almost lunchtime, are you sure you won't stay for some food?'

Joe shook his head. 'I'd better get back. I'll take a sandwich with me, though.'

'Hang on.' I took hold of his arm to stop him walking away. 'Is there any evidence that Philippa got up during the night? Did any staff see her go to the bathroom?'

Joe pulled out his notebook and started flicking through the small pages.

'I think she did… yes. The warder in the room remembers her going because she was one of the loudest snorers. He said there was a brief respite from the noise when she went to the toilet. The warder downstairs didn't see her; he was walking someone to the gents' toilet around the same time, which was in the opposite direction.'

'Do you think she could have done it – killed Thomas, I mean – if she thought it was Conrad?'

Joe didn't look sure. 'I didn't think so, not until you told me about her little shrine. Now she's high on my list of suspects. But we don't have any evidence to tie her to the scene of the murder.'

'Maybe you'll find something when you pay her a visit. Perhaps she's kept a souvenir of the event.'

'You mean like a severed ear? I didn't know you were the gruesome type. Anyway, the body was intact.'

'No, I don't mean that. Maybe she took something from the breakroom – a handkerchief, something like that.'

Joe pulled his jacket on. 'Not impossible. We'll find it if she did. What sandwich do you recommend? I'm starting to get hungry.'

19

I watched Mark as he spoke to a group of tourists. They were wrapped up against the cold as he pointed out some of the architectural features in the courtyard. You could see evidence of the original Tudor building here, and the cobbles underfoot helped you feel like you'd gone back in time, but I knew Mark would be trying to keep this part of the tour short. It was too cold to be out here for long. The sky was a steel grey and the air felt damp. It was the kind of cold that seeped into your bones and required a long steaming-hot bath if you were to stand any chance of feeling warm again.

Pat from security walked past the group, the large set of keys that hung from his belt jangling as he went. He made no effort to silence them. Then he spotted me and walked over.

'Imagine paying good money to stand in the cold on a day like this. Crazy.' He was wearing gloves, but was still rubbing his hands together to keep warm.

'What are you doing here? I thought you were on nights.'

'I am, but the police wanted another word with me and Rog, so we both decided to hang around, get some overtime in.'

I looked in the direction of the group. 'Mark'll take them inside as soon as he can.'

'Has your mate Joe told you how the police are gettin' on?' He continued to watch the group, his eyes following them as they walked to another corner of the courtyard. 'That Harnby doesn't give anything away.'

'Not really,' I lied. 'I just keep him topped up with coffee.'

'Hmm, well, I'll be glad when it's done. We've still got press sniffing around and getting in the way, and there's a couple of police cars blocking up the back lane. Dunno what we're going to do if we have to get a fire truck down there.'

He didn't seem to be in any kind of a hurry, so I thought I'd take the opportunity to see if he knew anything helpful.

'Thomas Hattersley's dad used to work here, did you know him?'

'He didn't exactly work here; he helped out when we used to have shoots, but we're talkin' thirty years back. Cash-in-hand work, nothing serious. They were a bad lot, though, the whole family. It's hard to feel sorry for Thomas, he was no better than the rest of them.'

Pat's eyes followed the group as they went under a stone archway and through a worn wooden door that looked as old as the cobbles.

'Did you know him, then? Thomas, I mean.'

'Nah, it all kicked off a couple of years before I got here, but I 'eard all about it. I like to keep my ear to the ground, always have. You don't know what's going to come in handy, and in this job, you need to be well informed. We have the security of this place to think about and I've always taken that very seriously.' As he spoke his final words, he seemed to grow a little taller and puff his chest out. He'd always had an air of self-importance about him, and I'd just witnessed it take a physical form.

'But Thomas seemed to have left that behind him and done quite well for himself. A respectable job, a love of history.'

'People like that don't change. Once a bad 'un, always a bad 'un. I'm sure that Douglas agrees with me.'

I spun my head round to face him. 'Douglas? Why Douglas? Did he know Thomas?'

'I don't know if he knew him as such, but they certainly had words that night. I saw them arguing after everyone had gone to bed. If you're doing your Miss Marple act again then you ought to talk to him.'

Douglas had claimed never to have met Thomas before the sleepover, and yet they were arguing. Either Douglas was lying, or they'd found a way to annoy each other very quickly. Pat was turning out to be useful. For all his arrogance, he had been here for years and probably had a mine of amazing information in that head of his. I wouldn't dismiss him quite so quickly next time.

Mark looked frozen as he walked into my office. I had a moment of panic, but then realised that his birthday cake, which I'd yet to finish, was under a box and out of sight. I scooted my chair against the far wall, which in practice meant I'd moved about a foot, and Mark shoved some papers aside before sitting on my desk. He didn't attempt to remove his coat.

'I should be spending my birthday on a tropical island some-where, not freezing my digits off with a bunch of hungover architecture students.'

'Was that the group I saw you with?'

'Probably, yeah. They were alright, but one of them admitted to me that they'd been on a bit of a bender the night before, so I was lucky they stayed awake. I don't know why I bother sometimes.'

'Because you love it,' I told him firmly. 'Besides which, you've been in their shoes on plenty of occasions, so you can't be too annoyed.'

'Me? Hungover? How dare you! Not since, ooh, the weekend before last.' He grinned. 'So, how's my cake coming along?' He glanced over his shoulder in the direction of the box.

'I have no idea what you're talking about. Have you finished that manuscript yet?' I asked, hoping to distract him.

'I have.'

'Were there any revelations?"

'No, it continued in the same vein. It's well written, a lot of the information reasonably well known already, but it will make a good addition to the books about the history of the family. It looks like it's finished, apart from the bibliography and author bio. There are a number of notes that reference books that aren't listed, so I reckon whoever it belonged to was still working on it.'

'Joe told me that Thomas would look over manuscripts for people, a sort of unqualified editor. Do you think it belongs to a client rather than him?'

Mark nodded. 'That would make sense, but there's nothing to give away who the author is, if it's not Thomas. One thing did cross my mind, though.'

He paused for too long. I didn't have the patience for his amateur dramatics today, birthday or not.

'Get on with it.'

'Who do we know that is going on endlessly about a book he's writing – a book about Charleton – and whose work, if his tour performances are anything to go by, is going to need plenty of help?'

'Douglas. Of course.' I stood up. In the tiny space, we were nose to nose as I reached around Mark for my coat, which was hanging on the back of the door.

'Where are you going?'

'Where are *we* going. Come on, we're going to talk to Douglas, and I'll fill you in on the chat I had with Philippa this morning.'

'But I've still not defrosted,' he whined, 'and it's my birthday. Wait, what about Philippa?'

'Then you'll acclimatise back into the cold quicker,' I reasoned. I knew curiosity would get the better of Mark if I mentioned I'd spoken to Philippa. 'Out of my way, birthday boy.'

Mark's office was deserted. There was no sign of Douglas or the other two tour guides who had desks in the room. Making my way straight to Douglas's desk, I started to go through the piles of paper that littered it. I guessed that he must have his own system of filing, but there was no way I could tell what it was.

'What are you doing?' Mark exclaimed.

'There might be other printouts, copies of sections of the book, something you recognise from the manuscript that ties it to him.'

'Why don't we just ask him?'

I looked around the room. 'I don't see him, and I'm not waiting. Besides which, he claimed that he'd never seen Thomas before Saturday night, but he was seen arguing with him by Pat, so I doubt we'd get the truth from him.'

'Well noted, someone's on the ball. Surely there'll be a copy on his computer.' Mark leant over me and switched the computer on. As it starting humming into life, he pulled off his coat and sat down at the desk.

'It'll be password protected, especially if there's stuff he wants to hide.'

'True, but he complains every time the IT department emails to tell us to change our passwords. He asked me to log on for him once when he was working from home and send a document to him. I just need to remember what it was. You know, I still can't believe you went to see Philippa without me.' He looked at me and shook his head.

'Focus, man,' I said, pointing at the computer.

He stared at the screen until it blinked into life, and then tried a couple of different words.

'I remember it was the name of his dog, and…'

'If he comes in, there'll be hell to pay. Do you know where he is?'

Mark didn't look up. 'No idea.'

I dived into stacks of paper and flipped through files, but there was nothing.

'Hang on, he was shredding stuff yesterday. What if that was it?'

'Then it's shredded and we'll have no idea. Buster, Bobby, Billy…' Mark was pounding on the keys.

'What if it's not completely destroyed?' I'd heard of crimes that had been solved because someone painstakingly recreated documents from their shredded remnants. Grabbing the shredder, I lifted the lid, pulled out a handful of paper and put it on the desk. If we could tie Douglas to Thomas via the manuscript, then we had another solid lead.

'Are you completely out of your mind? How much coffee have you had today?'

'Enough to know we can do this. Come on.'

He didn't move from his seat, just kept trying different passwords.

'Firstly, it's my birthday, which means I should be spending the day being waited on hand and foot, and secondly, this is going to be like looking for dandruff in a snowstorm. Not possible and not much fun… Got it, Bertie, and then its age. Douglas just kept upping that number with each password change.'

'Alright, old man, get on with it.'

I stared at the screen as Mark took us through a series of folders, the only noise in the room the click of a computer mouse. Then the quiet was interrupted by the sound of Douglas's voice over the radio.

'Security, this is Art Tour 1, this is Art Tour 1. Just to let you know I've finished the last tour of the day and the Long Gallery is locked and secure.'

'Thank you, Art Tour 1,' came the reply.

Mark and I looked at each other, and then scrambled into action. He rapidly closed down files, while I madly stuffed paper back into the shredder bin. I couldn't help but giggle.

'What are you laughing at? I'm the one that has to share an office with him if he finds us.'

'Sorry, I can't help it, we must look ridiculous.'

'You look ridiculous, fighting with that stuff. There's bits all over the floor.'

On my hands and knees, I started trying to pick up all the tiny bits of paper I could.

'Come on, he won't notice that.'

We ran to the door, down the stairs and into the courtyard, where Mark came to a sudden stop.

'Why are we running? That's my office too. We could have just moved to my desk.'

I gasped for breath; I wasn't used to taking exercise.

'Good point. Would have been... a better point... if you'd said... it in there,' I replied in between gulps of air.

'Any errors of judgment can be forgiven on my birthday.'

'You and your bloody birthday.'

'Did someone not get enough sleep?'

'No. What next?'

'Come with me, I've got an idea.'

'I should get back to the café. You're welcome to join me and spend what is left of the working day skiving in a corner, making snarky comments at my staff.'

'Marvellous. Throw in a chocolate brownie and I'm in, only I'm going to use your computer.'

I looked his skinny frame up and down. He seemed to spend half his life eating cakes and pastries, but there wasn't an ounce of fat on him. I, on the other hand, only had to inhale a whiff of freshly baked cookies and I could feel my hips expanding.

We pulled up our collars and braced ourselves against the rain that was starting to fall in big bloated drops.

I set Mark up in my office with cake and coffee. He told me he needed an hour to pursue an idea he had. After half an hour of cleaning tables, loading the dishwasher and generally getting under Tina's feet, I couldn't wait any longer. I pushed my way into the office.

'Budge up.'

'Hang on.' Mark shuffled the chair as far as he could. 'I'm not done yet.'

'I want an update, so you better not be online shopping for a new set of curtains.'

He turned and stared at me. 'Curtains? Why would I want curtains?'

'I dunno, it was the first thing that came to mind.'

He turned back to the screen. 'You worry me. I'm using the online archives of the British Library. I often use them as a resource when I'm researching tours. Most people don't realise what you can get access to without leaving the comfort of your own home.'

He was tapping and scrolling like his life depended on it; he knew what he was doing. I'd still be trying to log on, even after half an hour.

'I've only found three so far, but I'm right. Look.'

He held up a page of the manuscript against a paragraph of text he'd highlighted on the screen. I read one, then the other. They were the same, almost word for word, just a couple of minor changes here and there.

'What am I looking at?'

Mark swivelled the office chair round so he was facing me.

'Thomas has highlighted certain passages, like this one. He's noted the name of the book it's taken from. Those books don't appear in the manuscript's bibliography and I imagine they were never going to be added. My guess is that whoever wrote this was plagiarising texts and hoping no one spotted it. None of them are popular books, they're all pretty old and difficult to get hold of. It's unlikely they appear on any university reading list, and I would imagine there aren't many people around who remember them or have copies. Of course, if you know exactly what you're looking for, it's really not that hard to find, but no one would have known to look. But Thomas knew his stuff. He's also a details man. If he got wind of a problem, he would have hunted it down.'

I playfully punched Mark on the shoulder. 'You're not as green as you're cabbage looking. So, now we need to prove who wrote the manuscript. Are you still convinced that it's the work of Douglas?'

'I'm more convinced than ever. We know he's lazy when it comes to the behind-the-scenes stuff, so he's bound to take a shortcut if he can. I also reckon he's daft enough – or maybe naïve or arrogant enough, depending on how you look at it – to think he could get away with it. Come on, get your coat on. You're at risk of being demoted to Watson status.'

20

The rain hadn't let up as we walked quickly across the courtyard. In the distance, I could see a hunched figure, equally bundled up against the cold, make its way towards the staircase that led up to the live interpreters' breakroom. I was struggling to make out who it was as the rain ran down my glasses and turned everything into a grey misty blur.

'Wasn't that Douglas?'

'It was. Come on, we need a word with our soon-to-be-published history writer.'

I hadn't returned to the breakroom since yesterday morning when I'd found Thomas's body. The worn wooden staircase and roughly painted corridors now seemed eerie and the atmosphere still and cold. It hadn't always felt that way, and I knew logically that nothing had changed, but a little part of me wondered if I was going to stumble on another disturbing scene.

We climbed slowly, carefully placing our feet to avoid any creaking planks of wood – a largely pointless exercise. Winding our way up two floors, we stood outside the breakroom. The entrance was actually two large wooden doors, the kind you could burst through to make a dramatic entrance, and one was slightly ajar. We could hear a scrabbling inside – a chair moving, a drawer being opened. I stepped closer and peered through the gap. Douglas was looking for something and muttering to himself.

A wave of tiredness swept over me. This was not where I wanted to be right now; I was low on patience.

'Douglas.' I stepped into the room with a determination to get this over with.

'Soph…' It seemed I'd taken Mark by surprise, and he was still outside the door as I reached the middle of the room.

'Lost something, Douglas? Do you need a hand?'

'What? I… no.' He stood up, guilt and surprise plastered across his face as he looked back and forth between the two of us.

'You know the police have been over this place multiple times. If you've lost something, they're bound to have it.'

Just the thought of that seemed to horrify him. I was painfully aware of the desk and chair to my left, sitting in front of a window that looked out over the gardens to the side of the house. Less than forty-eight hours ago, I had found Thomas's body slumped over that very same desk, but right now, that didn't seem quite so important.

'Are you looking for this?' Mark stepped forward, holding a large brown envelope in the air. I hadn't realised he'd brought his bag with him, but I was glad he had. It made for a fabulously dramatic moment, and was just Mark's style.

'I… I don't know what it is, what you're talking about.' Douglas didn't take his eyes off the envelope; he knew very well what it contained. He straightened himself up as though trying to project an air of confidence. 'I'm just looking for some paper-work I might have left here. Nothing important.'

'What time were you here until on Saturday night?' I asked, wondering if I could get anything out of him. 'I know you didn't go straight home after you finished the tour.'

'No, of course not, you saw me at the Dickens reading. I

stayed to chat to the guests, and then left as they started going to bed.'

That didn't match with what Pat had said, and for all his bluster and arrogance, I was inclined to believe Pat.

'You were seen later than that, and I'm guessing that security can confirm what time you left the house. If that's what you told the police, then it won't be long before they work out that your story has some big holes in it.'

He looked briefly nervous, but seemed to gather himself and made for the door.

'I'm wondering what Thomas was doing with this?' Mark had stepped into Douglas's path and made to open the envelope. 'The more I read it, the more I recognise the style, or some of it at least.'

'I still don't know what you're talking about.' Douglas no longer sounded so sure of himself. 'It's not my manuscript.'

'How do you know there's a manuscript in here?' Mark feigned surprise. 'It could be a magazine article, a blog post. I never said it was a manuscript.'

Douglas was looking increasingly lost.

'For heaven's sake, Douglas!' I snapped, taking him by the arm and steering him to the sofa. 'Sit down.'

Mark looked wide-eyed at me.

'What? I'm tired, I've had too much coffee and he's starting to irritate me.'

Douglas made to get up, but I glared at him and he stayed where he was.

'Mark's read the manuscript. We know you're writing a book, you can't stop talking about it...'

'And,' Mark interrupted, 'now I think about it, this is definitely written by the same hand as those articles that appear under your name in this.' He reached for one of the history magazines that sat on a coffee table – I recognised it as the one Mark had been reading in the café. He opened it up and pointed at a page. 'This is your work, right?'

'Yes,' Douglas replied hesitantly. Mark turned to me.

'It's the same author, I'd put money on it.' He looked back at Douglas. 'So, if you wrote this article, you wrote this book. Well, most of it.'

'It's not finished, there's still a lot of work to be done. I'd like it back.' He stared at Mark and reached for the envelope, but Mark didn't move. Douglas went quiet and sat back in the sofa. 'I haven't finished it, Thomas didn't give me a chance.'

'But you told me that you'd never met him before the night of the sleepover, that you didn't know him. Why didn't you want us to know you were working with him? I assume he's editing your book, or at least giving it a once-over before it goes to your publisher.' I couldn't understand what the problem was with Douglas admitting he knew Thomas.

'Thomas spotted something, didn't he? Something you hoped you'd get past everyone? Correct me if I'm wrong, but I reckon those books that aren't in the bibliography were never going in, were they? Thomas spotted some familiar passages. I'm sure a lot of this is your own work, but there are places where you've just stolen someone else's. You've got a track record, after all.'

'What are you talking about?' Douglas glanced back and forth between us both, eyes wide. He was starting to sweat.

'The Vogler Award.' I was seeing the same links that Mark had spotted. 'That time you paid someone else to write the essay, took the easy route. You knew winning would give you the exposure you wanted. This time, you just took someone else's work and Thomas spotted it. After getting away with something similar once, you thought you'd try it again. But you hadn't realised just how in-depth his knowledge and reading was. Have you really got a publishing deal?'

Douglas looked up. 'Yes. I returned the signed contract to them on Friday, and then Thomas called. Threatened to tell them. I'm an okay writer; I could manage a couple of articles, but

I just kept getting stuck. I'd run out of ideas. There was never enough for a book, and I was going to lose the contract. No one else wanted to take me on, this was my only chance. I thought no one would spot it. I needed this, I knew it would help my career.'

'Is that why Thomas kept leaving the activities on Saturday night?' I asked. Each time I'd seen him outside or at the back of a room, I'd just thought he'd wanted some fresh air, or didn't want to join in. Now I remembered Douglas arriving breathless as Dickens was reading from *Oliver Twist*, moments after I'd seen Thomas through the window, in the courtyard.

'Yes. He kept pestering me all night.' I could see the colour rising in Douglas's cheeks; he was getting riled. I wondered if we were about to see a display of the kind of temper that could lead to murder.

'Was that what you were seen arguing about later?'

He nodded, his hands fidgeting in his lap and his gaze occasionally lingering on the envelope that Mark still had in his hands.

'He would have destroyed me, I'd have lost the book deal and no one would have touched me again. I told him I was sorry, I'd rewrite it, make sure it was all my own work, but he was furious.' Douglas was angry himself now and just let it all spill out. 'People kept seeing us talking, but he wouldn't back off. I knew the breakroom would be empty, so I brought him up here where we wouldn't be seen and tried to talk him round. He wouldn't take no for an answer. Even when I offered him money, he wouldn't accept it, said I'd got the book deal under false pretences. I didn't know what to do.'

He stopped suddenly. I finished for him.

'So you killed him.'

'No! God, no, I didn't, I couldn't.' He sounded angry, but now there was a hint of desperation in his voice. 'We argued, I grabbed him, there was a bit of pushing and shoving, but I couldn't even hit him. I left him in here and went home, drank a bottle of wine, and eventually fell asleep. I had no idea he was dead until I got a message off a colleague. I know you've been involved in this sort of thing before, Sophie, you have to help me. I didn't do it.'

I glanced over at Mark, who shrugged his shoulders. I didn't know whether or not to believe Douglas. He'd certainly shown a full range of emotions and it was easy to imagine him losing his temper. Plus he was desperate and I knew that could make people do crazy things.

Mark stood up. 'You know the police have seen this already,' he brandished the envelope containing the manuscript again, 'they know it exists, and I'll need to tell them everything.'

'No you don't, not yet. Can't you wait, give them more time to find the killer?'

'And give you the chance to do a runner? I don't think so.'

Douglas glared at Mark. 'I told you, I didn't do it.'

'We can't promise anything, Douglas, I'm sorry. But if there's nothing to tie you to the murder, you'll be fine.'

I'd tried to sound soothing, but I realised it just sounded hollow. Mark looked at me and nodded in the direction of the door. I followed his lead and we left a dejected-looking Douglas on his own.

'You're a feisty little ankle biter,' Mark said as we made our way down the stairs.

'I'm tired, plus I don't think he's the strongest of characters, so I figured if I pushed him, it would all come spilling out of him.'

'What next?' he asked.

'We find Harnby and tell her everything.'

We didn't get very far. A bloody-nosed Conrad came round the corner, trying to stem his nosebleed with a handkerchief. The knuckles of his hand looked red and sore.

'You've been in the wars,' Mark observed.

'It's nothing, I'm just going to clean up. Is the breakroom open again?'

'It is, but you should have someone take a look at that.' I moved towards him, but he backed off.

'It's fine, just leave it.'

'Did you walk into a wall?' Mark asked with exaggerated innocence.

'I walked into a Duke.'

'You did *what*?' I tried to imagine the Duke of Ravensbury taking a swing at a member of staff. Conrad spotted my confusion.

'No, Harvey Graves. He said it's my fault that Lycia has dumped him. Didn't give a damn that I'm her actual husband. I went for him. If he hadn't got involved, we'd still be working it out and our marriage might have had a chance.'

'Where's Harvey now?' I hoped he wasn't bleeding to death somewhere in a darkened corridor.

'Security had hold of him, told me to make a swift exit and they'd send him home. Said they wouldn't tell the police and would put it down to the stress of recent events. I just want to go and get cleaned up.'

He walked past us and up the stairs. Mark watched him intently.

'If he's anything to go by, Harvey has a mean right hook, and quite a temper. Do you think he...'

'Killed Thomas thinking it was Conrad? He's been on my list since we found the body, and I might have overheard him confessing to the killing.'

Mark raised his eyebrows at me. 'You *what*?'

'Oh yeah, I haven't told you that bit.' I went on to fill him in on the argument I'd overheard between Harvey and Lycia, this time including the fact I was disturbed by Seth before I'd had a chance to hear the crucial words from Harvey. Mark was so deep in thought, he didn't even give me a hard time about having been caught in a compromising position by the gamekeeper.

'Put him up at the top of that list, young lady. I know security said they wouldn't tell the police about the fight between Conrad and Harvey, but I reckon I should give that brother-in-law of mine a call.'

I didn't get much closer to my office before I heard my name being called. It was the Duke – the real one. Dressed in a dinner jacket, he looked like an aging James Bond. Suave and debonair were two words that came to mind.

'Sophie, I found something you might be interested in. I have an old *Year in the Life of Charleton House* book from decades ago. It doesn't mention the Hattersleys, but the gamekeeper is featured in it. There are some marvellous old photos. I've left it with Gloria so you can collect it anytime. I must dash – I'm a brand ambassador for a whisky and they're dragging me along to some dinner. I've told the Duchess not to wait up.'

He grinned like a cheeky schoolboy and set off at a quick pace that I couldn't have kept up with if I'd tried. I blame my short legs, not my lack of exercise over the years. It amused me to think of photographs from the nineties as old; it was a sure sign I was getting on myself.

I thought about what the Duke had just told me. Gloria, the Duke and Duchess's personal assistant, is a terrifying woman of mature years who could give Joyce a run for her money. I briefly thought about putting off seeing her until the morning, but common sense got the better of me and I decided to get it over with. If facing Gloria could throw some light on recent events, then it was worth a moment of feeling like a terrified schoolgirl in front of a formidable headmistress.

21

*G*loria Dewhurst's office is really an alcove in a corridor. Her desk is stationed outside the door to the office the Duke and Duchess share, and no one has access to them without first being vetted by Gloria. I presume that she takes coffee and lunchbreaks, holidays, leaves early for dentist appointments or to take her car to the garage, like most people, but I have never seen her away from her desk, nor has anyone else I have spoken to. I wouldn't have been surprised to discover that she sleeps there. No piece of mail reaches the Duke and Duchess without first being inspected by her. She receives every phone call and decides who gets to be put through. I have heard a rumour that the Duke tried to have a direct line put into his office, but Gloria objected and he was too afraid to argue. I doubt the Queen is quite so well guarded.

Gloria wears her glasses on a chain around her neck, slowly placing them on the bridge of her nose to scrutinise whoever is standing across from her. Her loosely curled grey hair remains exactly the same, day after day, as does the string of pearls she wears and the bottle-green polo-neck sweater, no matter what time of year it is. Having never seen her stand, I have no idea how tall she is, and the only way we would find out her age would be to cut off a limb and count the rings. The woman is a mystery.

I arrived to find her tapping away on her keyboard. Her fingers froze above the keys as I walked around the corner and she reached for her glasses.

'Sophie Lockwood, I believe this is for you.' One hand moved swiftly and reached for a brown envelope at her side. She remained in pause mode while I opened it. 'Do you have everything you need?'

'Yes, yes thank you, Gloria.' I was about to walk away when I thought she might be able to help. 'Actually, I was wondering, do you remember Bernie Stubbs? He used to be a gamekeeper here.'

'Of course I remember him.' It was clearly a very stupid question.

'I believe there was a bit of an incident with some poaching?' Silence. 'Do you remember anything about it?'

'I'm not one to dwell on the past, nor do I engage in tittle-tattle… However, there was a very difficult period for Bernie, which I'm sure is on record somewhere. The current Duke's father was well aware of my feelings at the time, and that it was not one of his most auspicious moments. But he did the best he could with the information he had. Bernie's reputation remained an extremely positive one.'

'But didn't he retire early?'

'He did.' For a moment, I thought I glimpsed a flash of sympathy. 'The poor man was exhausted and wanted to spend time with his family. Now, if there's anything else you wish to know about his departure, then I would imagine that Human Resources are the people to talk to. Although I doubt there's anything they can tell you. I'm sure anything else remains confidential.'

'Of course. Thank you, you've been very helpful.'

She waited until I was out of sight round the corner before I heard her start typing again. That had been a painless encounter, but then I hadn't been trying to get beyond her to the Duke or

Duchess without an appointment. I decided I'd send up some pastries for her in the morning. Keep your friends close and your enemies closer.

I'd planned on returning to my office, but before I turned in through the door to the café, loud, angry shouting led me down the dark stone corridor that staff could take as a shortcut into the back lane. Harvey was still trapped against the wall by Pat, who was continuing to try to calm him down.

'I'll let you go when I know you're not going to do anything stupid.'

Harvey wasn't trying too hard to escape, but then Pat presented quite a barrier. In fact, Harvey looked more frustrated than violent; I doubted he would have run if he'd been freed. Even from the other side of the lane, I could see a smear of blood below Harvey's nose and more on his white shirt.

Lycia was over by the security gate, talking to Roger before walking off in the direction of the car park. He didn't look any more cheerful than he had the last time I'd seen him, and it seemed that Lycia was done with men fighting over her. It was hard to feel sympathy for her. If she didn't want to continue trying to repair the relationship with Conrad, she should have told him. She should have also been more upfront with Harvey, not given him hope, making the whole situation even more murky in the process.

I looked intently at Harvey. Was he really capable of murder? I had no idea if the police viewed him as a possible suspect.

I watched as the security gates rose into the air and an unmarked police car was let through to park across from my office windows. DS Harnby got out of the car and spoke to Roger. She followed up with a quick word with the officer who had been driving the car, who then walked over to Harvey. Pat stepped away and ambled back into the office. Security's plan of keeping the fight from the police had just fallen through.

'I was on my way back to the station when I got a call to

return. They're like kids. Did you witness the fight?' Harnby was standing next to me.

'No. I ran into Conrad on his way to clean up; he was a bit of a mess.'

She nodded, but didn't look at me, her eyes still trained on her officer and Harvey.

'Does this push Harvey up the list of suspects?'

'You know I can't answer that, Sophie, but he's not doing himself any favours.' I wondered if Joe had updated her following my conversation with him. She appeared to take a moment to think before asking her next question. 'You found the body. Do you really think someone could have mistaken Thomas for Conrad, got close enough to kill him and still not realised?'

As much as I didn't want to, I ran back through the events of the morning when I had found Thomas. I had assumed it was Conrad, but then I hadn't got too close.

'Possibly. It would have been pretty dark. The only lamp was a small Anglepoise in the far corner. Everything about him screamed Charles Dickens. He was wearing the same kind of coat and shirt. From behind, you couldn't see that he had on a much plainer waistcoat. Their hair is similar, he was surrounded by Dickens's props. If you were in a rage, then I guess you might see what you wanted to see.'

I had seen the geranium on the floor, the book and the hat on the table, and that had been it. As far as I knew, I had been looking at a dead Charles Dickens. Once I'd reached that conclusion, I didn't hang around long enough to double-check.

'You have a reputation for being quite good at this sort of thing, Sophie, do you have any ideas?'

I looked up at DS Harnby; she looked tired. Since we had first been introduced, I'd done a good job of avoiding her, mainly because I knew she didn't approve of me sticking my nose in, and I didn't feel like getting a lecture that I would find harder to ignore than Joe's friendly warnings. But this time, something felt different. I saw a woman in a really tough job who was probably being watched closely by senior officers and could never relax, not for a moment.

'I have ideas, but I also have some information. Come on, I'll make you a drink.'

'Coffee, or is it too late in the day?'

'It's never too late in the day. Black, please. So what do you have to tell me?'

DS Harnby was standing by the counter as I made her coffee. The café was closed and the team had done a swift job of clearing up and heading home. I had flicked on a couple of lights as it was already dark outside and the café was gloomy and grey, but I couldn't be bothered taking any of the upturned chairs off the tables, so I grabbed some stools and we sat at the counter.

'Has Douglas Popplewell been on your radar?' I asked.

'He's appeared on it, but then so have you. You did find the body.' She smiled. I hadn't expected her to say that out loud, even though I knew it to be true. She was trying to keep me on my toes.

'Fair enough. It seems he had a lot of dealings with the deceased.'

I was telling her about Thomas and his link to Douglas, coming to the end as Mark walked in.

'Roger said he'd seen you both head this way. Detective Sergeant, hello.'

'Mark. Sophie's just been filling me in. Do you want to tell me about the manuscript?'

Mark's eyes lit up. He loved talking about research, books, the house – you name it. If DS Harnby wanted a brief summation, she was about to be disappointed.

I left them to it.

22

I wanted to try to get my thoughts together, but the café was starting to feel too closed in. I felt like I'd spent far too much time in there over the last couple of days; I was used to being out and about, attending meetings, visiting the other cafés. It was still less than forty-eight hours since the sleepover began, but it seemed like an eternity, and as though I hadn't left the place in a week.

There was no point going home before Mark's birthday dinner at the pub. I could fill my time with paperwork, but first I wanted some fresh air. It was dark, but there was enough light coming from the house to allow me to take one of the short walking routes that had become a favourite when I needed thirty minutes away from either my team or a tray of burnt cookies.

Pat was standing at the security gate, a bouquet of autumnal flowers in his hands, the oranges, greens and reds a burst of colour in the diminishing light.

'Very pretty, Pat. You got a secret admirer?'

'They're for the Duchess, she gets 'em all the time. They're probably for opening a supermarket or somethin'.'

'What are we meant to do with those?' Roger had appeared by

Pat's side. "Spose it's our job to get them delivered, like we've not got enough to do. Give me that.' Roger roughly took the flowers from Pat and marched back into the office. Pat watched him leave, and then turned to me.

'Rog has a lot on his mind. He's a bit... distracted.'

'Is he okay? Has something happened?'

'It's not my place to say. It's his business, but I didn't want you to think his mood was aimed at anyone in particular.'

'Okay, thanks, Pat.'

'I'll keep an eye on him, don't you worry.'

I turned to set off on my walk. Maybe Pat did have a heart after all.

My route took me through the walled garden I had seen Lycia and Harvey in, across the top of the car park and round the back of the stable block. From there, it was a quick ten-minute pull up a steep, wide path to a folly that overlooked the house. Follies were never built to serve a purpose, extravagant garden ornaments that were just fun to look at and demonstrated the owners wealth; this one was a twenty-foot tower that afforded wonderful views over the estate, it was decorated with finials in the shape of pineapples along the edge of the roof. Pineapples had been a rare delicacy in the 18th century and a symbol of power and wealth, perfect for the Fitzwilliam-Scotts.

A weather vane, also in the shape of a pineapple, sat on the roof. The spiral staircase that took visitors to the top was closed to the public, but in warmer weather, Mark and I had come here with a bottle of champagne and a promise to Roger that I'd bake him a cake if he would slip us the key to the gate at the bottom of the stairs and keep our little adventure to himself. It was hard to imagine him doing us that kind of favour today.

I dragged my tired legs up the hill, panting and telling myself to do this more often, then my thoughts drifted back to Roger. His sullen mood was so out of character. We'd had a spate of dead bodies onsite over the last year, so it couldn't be the shock, unless it was all getting a bit much for him. He was such a good-hearted man, it was easy to imagine him finding evil acts difficult to stomach. Perhaps this recent case had upset him in particular.

Roger hadn't known the victim, as far as I was aware. His current state of mind meant that I didn't feel able to have a heart-to-heart with him – I instinctively felt it was best to leave him in peace. It had been good of Pat to tell me that I wasn't the cause of his bad mood, but still, it worried me.

I touched my hand to the cold stone, paused briefly to take in what little I could see of the view now the sun had gone down, shivered and immediately headed back down. The path was slippery and damp, so I stuck to the side and the longer grass as I half ran, half walked, not quite in control of my speed.

It felt wonderful to be out in the fresh air, to focus on something physical, instead of endlessly trying to solve the puzzle that surrounded Thomas. This was exactly what I needed. I ran the last few yards and tumbled into the rear wall of the stables, laughing to myself at the childish simplicity of it all. Now I just had to work my way through a couple of hours of rotas, holiday requests and emails, and then I would have nothing more challenging to face than which gin to choose off the menu at the Black Swan.

The car park was quiet; only a few staff cars remained. As I walked past one, I noticed that someone was sitting in the driver's seat; it was Lycia. She must have been there a little while. I knocked on the window.

'Are you okay?' She jumped, then wound her window down. 'Sorry, I didn't mean to startle you. Are you alright?'

She nodded. 'Yes, thanks, I'm just leaving.'

'Are you sure you're alright? You've been sat here a while, don't you want to go home?'

'No, I just needed time to think.'

'I couldn't help but overhear your conversation with Harvey earlier, in the garden.'

'How? I didn't see you.'

I remembered Seth finding me on the golf cart and decided not to answer that.

'Can we talk, just for a couple of minutes?' I was getting cold; the sweat I'd built up running down the hill was now making me shiver. Lycia nodded and I heard the click of the door lock. I walked round and got in the passenger seat. 'Thanks. This must have been a tough couple of days for you. Harvey can't be making it any easier.'

'No, but it's not his fault.'

'He really seems to like you. I guess he'd do anything for you.'

She looked at me intently. 'I think he probably would. He's a romantic and a gentleman, in the old-fashioned sense.'

'Do you think he'd kill for you?'

She laughed, and then quickly quietened down. 'You're serious?' She thought for a moment. 'You know, it crossed my mind – for a second, that's all. But Harvey could never do that. He's prone to grand displays of emotion, but he doesn't have what it takes to kill someone. I can't imagine him getting the two men mixed up, either. He knows Conrad too well, and as far as I know, he has no history with Thomas.' Warming to the subject now, she had turned to face me and stopped playing with her car keys.

'Did you know Thomas?' I asked.

'Only from the occasional event. He didn't go to many; I think he looked down on what we do, never really understood all the hard work and research that goes into it. I tended to avoid him, he just wasn't very pleasant. His wife Annie is lovely, though I have no idea what she saw in him. It was always a little more stressful when Thomas was around, and it was already bad enough when Philippa was there. Conrad had words with him a couple of times.'

She paused and looked out of the window before continuing.

'Conrad and I talked about moving when we decided to stay together. We could both find work elsewhere, especially in London, but we love it here. Derbyshire is our home.'

I could understand that. After all, I'd moved back here after ten years in London. It was my home, too.

Something she'd said reminded me of my conversation with Conrad.

'Conrad said he and Thomas had words on a few occasions, do you know why?'

'Thomas could be sarcastic. He'd try and test your knowledge, trip you up if he could, but he did it in a mean-spirited way, not like the visitors who do it in order to have some fun and maybe learn something at the same time. I think he just pushed Conrad too far on a couple of occasions.'

'This is rather a personal question, but I believe someone told you about Conrad and Philippa. Who was it?'

She nodded. 'I've always assumed someone wanted to make sure I knew, yes. A note had been dropped in the pocket of my costume. I found it later when I was getting changed. We were at a big event over at Berwick Hall. There was dancing and I spent a lot of time talking to the public. Thomas was definitely there, and at the next couple of events he seemed particularly smug, making comments about illicit liaisons and secrets. I wouldn't have been able to prove it, and anyway, it didn't seem important. Conrad and I just needed to try and work at fixing things.'

'Did you see Conrad after the gathering you all had on Saturday night? Do you know what time he left?'

'After he refused to come home with me, I left him in the security office with Roger, waiting for a taxi. I don't know what time the taxi picked him up, though.'

'And you just went home? How come the police were struggling to get hold of you the next day?'

'I was annoyed at Conrad for refusing to come home, so I

turned my phone off. I wanted some peace and quiet, time to think, and I guessed Harvey would start texting me.'

'What are you going to do now?'

'I don't know. I still love Conrad. Maybe we need to get away from here; maybe staying in Derbyshire wasn't the right thing. None of this is his fault, not this weekend. I've been stupid; I was leading Harvey on. He's uncomplicated. Conrad had been working so hard at being the perfect husband, but it just didn't feel relaxed, normal. I don't want us to give up, not yet.'

To me, it all sounded exhausting, and I briefly thanked my lucky stars that I was single. The most complicated relationship issue in my life was judging Pumpkin's mood swings; no wonder I was in no rush to get a boyfriend.

'I hope you figure it out. You should get home.'

Lycia nodded and started the engine. I got out of the car, resisting the urge to run back to the office. With any luck, Harnby would still be in the café. It was time to catch up with her.

23

*H*arnby had gone, so had Mark. I called Joe, but there was no answer so I left him a message. I doubted Roger's ability to register Conrad's whereabouts if he'd sat on his lap, but I wanted to be sure, and Joe would have seen Roger's statement. There was nothing I could do but wait.

I lifted the box that was covering Mark's cake and gave it a once-over. Dammit. I'd put a layer of fondant over the books and they now looked like worn leather, but that was as far as I'd got. While I prepared the icing so I could add titles, I started to run through everything in my head. I knew I wasn't thinking clearly; I hadn't had enough sleep, was still largely running on caffeine and had far too much information buzzing around my head, so I needed to try to make sense of it all.

Despite there only being one body, there were two potential victims. Conrad – I wasn't convinced that Philippa was involved. She was a spurned lover, but the more I thought about her pictures of Conrad, the more it seemed like a shrine to Charles Dickens. Maybe her interest wasn't really in Conrad, but the idea of him as someone else. Conrad didn't seem threatened by her and had said it could be nice to have her around: a fellow Dickens aficionado. Maybe it was Lycia's response that had turned all that into such a drama, rather than Philippa, who had simply continued attending events as normal.

Harvey was frustrated and passionate, his emotions running high, but if he had killed Thomas thinking he was Conrad, then I found it hard to imagine him starting a fight with Conrad in full view of anyone who wandered down the back lane. It was too risky. No, that was the overemotional response of someone who was running out of hope. I was doubting Douglas's involvement, too; he was naïve, but that wasn't a crime, and his attempt at plagiarism hadn't actually seen the light of day. He'd also been genuine when he'd pleaded with me to help him.

I tried to focus on the cakes in front of me; I couldn't get the decorative swirls consistent, and one was slipping off the book entirely. The gold letters in one title were getting smaller and smaller; I should have put a guide in place, but it was too late now.

Checking my phone, making sure the ringer was on full volume – I didn't want to miss Joe calling – I watched out of the window as Roger walked back to his office. He must have delivered the flowers to the Duchess; they'd been as beautiful as the ones Bill had bought for Mark. I couldn't remember the last time I'd been sent flowers.

I remembered the poor, lonely geranium I'd stood on in the breakroom and thought about Charles Dickens. Something was niggling at me. Thomas wasn't a popular man, but other than Douglas, I wasn't sure anyone hated him enough to kill him. And Douglas couldn't even find the strength to hit him. Someone had, though; someone had not only hit him, but stabbed him too. But Conrad had gone straight to the Black Swan, and everyone else had been caught up in their own dramas.

My wrist was aching and my hand was starting to shake; the writing was getting worse, but it was still legible – just. I was done, and anyway, it wouldn't take long for it to be devoured and all evidence of my artistic failings to vanish.

I threw everything in the sink and covered the cake; I'd tidy up tomorrow. Picking up my phone, I went to sit at my desk. It was covered in notes that my staff had left me: scraps of paper with requests for holiday, or shift swaps, or items of uniform that needed replacing. We had forms for all that and they knew it, but I was too tired to be cross.

I picked up one of the notes and folded it into tiny squares. Lycia had been given a note, and the one person who had been described as unpleasant was Thomas. If Thomas had given Lycia the note and Conrad had found out, then he had a reason to want him dead, but Conrad had gone to the Black Swan. He'd had drinks with his colleagues in his costume, so presumably he hadn't returned to the breakroom straight after the event to get changed, but he would have needed to return to get his wallet later. Conrad had told me he'd gone to the pub to spend the night, but he couldn't do that without his wallet – a wallet he wouldn't be allowed to have on him when he was performing and which he would have left in a locker, in the breakroom. He must have gone back and found Thomas where Douglas had left him, the geranium falling out of his buttonhole while he was up there.

My phone beeped. I grabbed it and read the message.

'On my way, stay put. X'. It was Joe. Okay, there was no need to rush.

My eye was caught by the envelope Gloria had given me that I'd tossed on the desk when I'd returned with DS Harnby. What did Bernie Stubbs have to do with all this, if anything?

I dialled Joyce's mobile; she picked up after two rings.

'This had better be good. No one disturbs my bubble baths, but I'll make an exception for you.'

I squeezed my eyes tight shut, trying to keep that image out of my head.

'You've worked here a while, Joyce.'

'That's putting it mildly. Some would say I was present when the foundations went down, but that's pushing it. Why?'

'Did you know Bernie Stubbs, the gamekeeper?'

'No, he was before my time – just. I remember it was my first week of work and I got left in the shop on my own as most people went to his funeral. You should ask Roger, he was here then. Been in his job a couple of years when I arrived.'

As she talked, I pulled the book out of the envelope. It was a large, slim hardback, more like a photo album.

'Okay, I will, thanks. See you later.'

She hung up. I flicked through the pages that captured food festivals, weddings, building renovations, lambing seasons, car shows and a visit by the Queen, turning to a page that had been marked for me by the Duke. There were photos of Bernie Stubbs. In one, he was feeding the deer; in another he appeared in a group shot with a couple of park rangers. They were lined up in front of their Land Rovers and pickup trucks, a very sweet-looking brown-and-white spaniel sitting at their feet, staring into the camera lens, its tongue hanging out.

I felt a stab of sympathy for Bernie. To have worked for thirty years in a job he loved, and then been falsely accused of an act so serious, he could have lost that job. He was a big, hearty chap, his ruddy cheeks and tough-looking skin a sign of the life he spent outdoors. His enormous hands were on his hips and he stood looking proudly into the camera, appearing approachable and friendly. I would have loved to have met him.

He also looked very familiar. I felt like I *had* met him, but I knew that was impossible. There was just so much about him that was recognisable, I expected to be able to look out of the window and watch him walk down the lane.

Then I realised I had, sort of.

I called the security office.

'Yes?' It was Roger. I paused, wondering if I should try to talk to him, but I'd seen something in the photos that was more pressing.

'Is Pat there?'

'No.'

'I just wanted a word with him, any idea where he might be?'

'He went to lock up the shop.'

'I'll track him down.'

He hung up.

The gift shop was deserted. All the lights were off, but an orange glow filtered in from the courtyard outside, the shelves and display cases taking on a ghostly quality. The outlines of the gifts and toys were unnerving, especially the dolls, or if faces from the front of books suddenly peered out of the gloom. I couldn't be sure I wouldn't walk into something at every turn.

Once the shop staff had left for the day, security would come and do another check. They'd also do patrols around the building throughout the night. Pat would be making the first patrol of the evening, ensuring none of the day staff had missed anything. There was no need for him to put the lights on; he would know the place like the back of his hand.

The steps into the shop are made of worn stone; hundreds of years of footsteps have left a big dip in the middle of every one. Barely a week goes by that someone doesn't trip over the 'mind your step' sign. The old door at the bottom looks like something left over from the Tudor period: dark wood with enormous metal hinges that takes two hands to push open. Fortunately it had already been open enough for me to slip through, so I didn't have to exert myself this late in the day.

'Pat? Pat, it's Sophie. Are you in here?'

There was a rustle in a far corner.

'Pat, is that you?'

The sound of a fire exit being tested was followed by a jangle of keys.

'Who's there?' Torchlight shone across the room and I squinted as it hit my eyes. 'Sophie, what are you doing here?'

'Looking for you, do you have a minute?'

'Not really, but you ask your questions while I finish up in here.'

I saw the outline of his bulky figure head towards Joyce's office.

'You've worked here a long time.'

'Twenty-five years give or take, one of the longest serving. Not like those just chasing their careers these days, here one minute, gone the next.' He gave the handle on Joyce's office door a turn. It was locked. He moved on. 'Why?'

'You said you knew of Arnold Hattersley, Thomas's dad. Did you ever meet him, or Thomas?'

I could trace Pat's movements by the noise of his footsteps as he walked the length of the shop. They came to a halt.

'Why would I have done? Like I said, it was before my time.'

'Yes, but you knew all about them, you saw them around. I just thought you might have come and visited Charleton House, especially when you had a family member working here. Didn't you come and see him? Join him on the job?'

He still didn't move. 'Whatcha talking about?'

'Bernie Stubbs. He's family, right?'

When I had looked at the book the Duke had left for me, there was no mistaking the similarity. The photo of Bernie would have been a spitting image of Pat, if Pat had bothered to get some fresh air and exercise. Pat's face had stared out at me from the ruddy cheeks and sun-worn skin. But it had been taken a very long time ago, and as Pat had said, a lot of staff had left since then.

'I know Thomas didn't work here, but did you come across him? He must have spent time with his dad.'

I heard Pat move and listened as his footsteps got closer. He was one of the few people who might have personal knowledge of what had happened all those years ago, and if it had any bearing on Thomas's death.

'Arnold was a waste of space. Did as little as he could, and then spent every penny he earnt down the pub. Bernie only used him when he had no choice, and anyway, it was a small community. You were meant to help each other out. Bernie was a good man, loyal. I wouldn't have bothered. I'd have got rid of Arnold. Better in the long run.'

I still couldn't make Pat out clearly. There was a fuzzy dark mass not far from me, but it was impossible to judge its distance. I moved away from the bottom of the stairs, trying to get a better view.

'Was Thomas involved in the poaching? He must have been eighteen at the time, old enough to get mixed up in it all.'

'Nah, he wasn't made of the right stuff. Always had his head in books. He'd even have one with him when he came down the pub. Thought he was better than the rest of us.'

'So you did meet him, then?' I listened intently as his story shifted, as the truth slowly came out.

The dark shape moved towards some windows to check they were locked. Then I lost sight of him behind the shelves.

'He could be a vindictive little sod, though.' There was a change in Pat's tone. He really didn't like Thomas. 'Once Uncle Bernie was suspended, I saw Thomas in the pub a couple of times. He always looked like he had a joke running through his head. A smirk on his face. Of course, now we know it's cos his dad was getting away with poaching, right under our noses. Arnold would be down the pub too, playing it all concerned, saying what a good man Bernie was, 'ow he loved workin' with him. Rubbish, all of it; he was gloating.'

Pat's voice had become harsher, the words spilling out of him, and I realised what an idiot I'd been. Pat, more than anyone, had reason to hold a grudge against Arnold, and by association, Thomas.

'Bernie was suspended from his duties for a whole year. Have you any idea how hard that was for him? He became a hermit. He was heartbroken.' Pat's voice was closer now, but I couldn't be sure which direction it was coming from. 'He loved this place, worked every hour God sent. He wanted to die on the job. Then it would have come to me.'

'What do you mean, come to you?'

'Bernie didn't have kids. In those days, family mattered, and without him having a son to take over the job of gamekeeper, I should have been next in line.' He was starting to raise his voice and I could tell that he was getting closer. I stepped backwards and hit the wall just to the side of the door, close enough to make a run for it.

'Why didn't you get the job?'

'After all that? Don't be stupid. There was still a cloud over our family name, they didn't want to touch us with a barge pole. The powers that be had been sniffing out candidates while Bernie was suspended. He hadn't even been found guilty and they were already thinking about who to replace him with. I reckon they were embarrassed, didn't want one of Bernie's relatives reminding them of how wrong they'd been. But it was mine by rights.'

I could feel the cold stone wall behind me. I knew Pat was close.

'But you are here, you still got a job.'

'As a bloody security officer, sure. I had to apply three times. Third time they had no excuse. I reckon they hoped I'd screw up, give them a reason to get rid of me. But I kept my nose clean, did a good job. I thought that once I was in, I could apply to be the gamekeeper when the new one left. I wanted to do it for Bernie, to get it back in the family. But no, they only went and gave the job to the new bloke's son. I didn't have a chance.

'To make things worse, he was a mate of Thomas's. My God, did Thomas gloat. Every time I went in the pub, he'd ask his mate how the job was going, full volume like. Make sure I heard. I stopped going in the end. They did the pub up, hold quizzes and all sorts now. Lost its spirit, not the place Bernie would have remembered.'

There was a very slight edge of sadness in his voice, but I didn't feel sorry for him. The more he said, the more I was certain that I was on my own in a darkened room with Thomas's killer.

'What happened at the weekend, Pat? Did Thomas say something to you?'

'He didn't have to. It took me a while to recognise him in that stupid get-up. Once he clocked me, that was it. Arrogant sod even raised his glass to me when I stuck my head in the door during dinner.

'I came across him when I was doing my rounds. He should have been sleeping, but he was in the breakroom at the desk. I don't know why he was there, but he was in a foul mood. Started winding me up about how I carried a torch instead of a gun, and no one would trust me with anything more lethal. I was on my way out, he didn't deserve my time, but he just couldn't keep his mouth shut.

'"Bernie would be *so* proud," he said. He was so smug. I grabbed the knife, and before he knew what was going on… He didn't have a chance to fight. I'm not sorry.'

I glanced over at the door, turning slowly, hoping he wouldn't realise what I was planning. But as I was about to move, he appeared from the shadows and I was within inches of his bloated body.

'Don't think you're going anywhere. I've got this far, I'll be here till the day I drop, just like Bernie wanted to.'

I ducked and made for the gap between Pat and the wall, but I wasn't quick enough and he moved. I slammed into his thigh. He shoved me back against the wall.

'I told you, you're going nowhere.'

'Roger knows I was looking for you.'

'Roger's an idiot, too bloody soft. Anyway, I finished checking the shop long before you arrived, didn't I. I never saw you.'

His hand was pressing my shoulder hard against the wall and it hurt like hell. I didn't see any alternative, so I shouted out, but the sound was cut off as his other hand, cold in its leather glove, folded itself round my neck. I started to choke.

'Don't be stupid. You might think you're something special round here, but not this time.' He added pressure. I wasn't sure if I was blacking out or staring into the gloom of the shop.

Before I could work out what was happening, the lights were thrown on and I was blinded by one of the ceiling spotlights pointing right over Pat's shoulder.

'What the hell?' Pat shouted, turning towards the door. As he turned, I made out the figure of Joyce, standing on the bottom step. She spun towards Pat, and in a sudden blur of movement I saw her leg fly up. Pat screamed. He let go of my neck and both his hands grabbed for his crotch, where Joyce's foot had landed with force.

'You bitch...' he cried out, his voice suddenly high pitched.

Joyce looked at me. 'See, I told you I could high kick with the best of them.'

24

'*I*'m so sorry, I'm so, so sorry.' Roger looked distraught. 'I couldn't forgive myself if something had happened to you.'

'It's okay.' I leant across Joe and took Roger's hand, giving it a squeeze. 'It's not your fault. Can you get me some water? I really need a drink.'

'I'll be right back.'

Roger hurried away. I looked at Joe.

'He's a sweet man, but I needed a break. It'll make him feel useful.'

'Something more serious could have happened, you know. If Joyce hadn't returned, you could be dead.'

Joe looked annoyed, but there was a softness in his voice. I rubbed my neck; it was still sore. We were sitting in the security office. Flashing blue lights cast a strange glow around the room, like an eerie disco. After Joyce had delivered a physical and emotional blow to Pat's manhood, we'd raised the alarm.

'What were you thinking?'

'I guess I wasn't. I just thought he might know something useful.'

Roger returned and handed me a glass. In his garbled apologies after the police had been called, he had admitted to being distracted the last couple of days, not picking up on signs that Pat might have been involved or realising that he didn't know where his colleague had been at key times on the night of the murder, missing discrepancies in Pat's statement. During the sleepover events, Roger had received a phone call telling him that his heavily pregnant daughter had been taken into hospital. I remembered him getting a phone call after he and Pat had been poking fun at the dancing.

'I wanted to go in and be with her, but my wife told me to stay here, that it would all be fine. The doctors just wanted to check and be sure that everything was okay. I knew I had a job to do here, I didn't want to let anyone down, but I couldn't think of anything else.'

That explained his bad mood over the last couple of days. I couldn't blame him; he doted on his daughter and was overjoyed at the thought of becoming a grandad.

'We got there in the end, Roger, that's all that matters.' I gave him the warmest smile I could manage.

'I'll give you some space, shout if you need anything, anything at all.'

If anyone needed anything, it was Roger. It was going to take a lot of cake and reassurance to help him lose the feeling of guilt he was carrying.

Another police car pulled up outside and the beam of the lights swung across the office walls. Joe looked out of the window.

'DI Flynn is here. Just in time to break the good news to the Duke, explain why you beat us to it, *again*.' The slight smile told me I wasn't in too much trouble. 'You better stay out of sight. I think Harnby is warming to you, but Flynn definitely isn't a fan.'

'Not a problem, I'll stay in here out of harm's way.'

'Great, now you decide to play it safe. Why didn't you do that with Pat?'

'Because I'd come to the conclusion it was Conrad who'd killed Thomas, so I didn't think Pat was a risk. Conrad said he'd gone directly to the Black Swan, that he'd decided to spend the night there. But he needed his wallet for that. He'd gone to the party straight from the reading, in costume. They're not allowed to have anything modern on them that's visible to the public and his wallet is a huge, bulky thing. That's why they have those little lockers in the breakroom, to keep their valuables safe. When Betsy arrived at the start of the evening to play the Duchess, she still had a watch on and I had to look after it for her.

'Conrad must have gone back to the breakroom after the party to get his wallet. I assumed that gave him the opportunity to run into Thomas after Douglas had left and kill him. He had motive enough. Conrad was hardly likely to tell us he'd been up there once he realised who the victim was, it would make him a suspect straight away. Add to that the punch that you said Thomas had received before he was killed. We know Douglas had been with Thomas, but when Mark and I confronted him, he said he'd been unable to hit him, so it wasn't him. I figured it was Conrad, mad at Thomas for vindictively letting Lycia know about his affair. He'd taken any control of the situation out of Conrad's hands.'

'But what about Philippa? It was thanks to your – well, Joyce's – concerns that we found her Conrad shrine.'

'Philippa was no longer a suspect in my mind when I realised that she was actually obsessed with Charles Dickens. Her interest in Conrad was secondary. She wasn't so fired up by passion that she was capable of killing him; the man she's crazy about is already dead. Apart from anything, if she had thought it was Conrad, killing him would deprive her of one of her favourite portrayers of Dickens. You haven't charged her with anything, have you?'

'No, unless a dubious taste in literature is a crime.'

I slapped his knee. 'Dickens was a genius. He wasn't such a great husband, I'll admit, but he had a rather natty taste in waist-coats, and he was a fan of gin.'

'That's all that matters, then. A gin drinker, he must be a good bloke. So let me get this straight. First Thomas has a barney with Douglas, who leaves him up in the breakroom. Next Conrad pitches up and smacks him because he made sure Lycia knew her husband had gone to a hotel with Philippa, and then Pat turns up and stabs him.'

'With his gloves still on,' I interjected, remembering the feel of the cold leather against my neck. Joe nodded.

'Thomas practically had a queue outside the door with a bone to pick – he wasn't a popular man.' He gave a wry smile. 'Come on, I'll ask someone to take you home so you can get changed and go to the pub. You can have your precious gin then.'

'I'm fine, I can drive. Are you coming?'

'Later, I have actually got a job to do.'

'I doubt Mark would consider tying up a murder case more important than his birthday, I'm just warning you.'

He laughed. 'I can't argue with that. Go on, drive safe.'

He kissed me on the cheek and was about to walk up the lane when I stopped him.

'Joe.' I took hold of his arm. 'You know they say police officers are getting younger every day?'

'Yes?'

'Well, it turns out they're getting hairier too.'

I pointed towards the open door of the nearest police car. Sitting in the driver's seat was a very confident-looking Romeo.

25

The Black Swan pub wasn't all that busy on the face of it, which wasn't surprising for a Monday. The noise emanating from a large table in front of the open fireplace, however, would have competed with any Saturday night. Bill and Father Craig Mortimer, the Charleton House chaplain, were debating the merits of two locally brewed stouts. Joyce was refilling her glass from a bottle of champagne and howling with laughter at something Bill had said. Mark, looking happy and relaxed, was chatting to Steve the landlord and ordering another bottle of wine. A number of birthday cards were standing in the middle of the table, their torn envelopes scattered around. A bottle of whisky in a gift box stood next to some books and a mug that declared 'I'm a tour guide. To save time, let's just assume I'm always right'. Wrapping paper had been screwed up into balls that were now strewn around like table decorations.

It was chaos. Wonderful, warm, loving chaos.

'SOPHIE! She's here, everyone.'

Bill jumped out of his chair and gave me a hug. 'Are you okay?' he whispered into my ear.

'I'm fine.' My hand instinctively went up to my neck. I had no idea if I'd bruise, but I'd worn a loose silk scarf just in case. 'A little sore, but nothing a gin and tonic won't solve.'

'Consider it done.' Bill went to the bar as Mark scraped his chair back and came over to give me an equally bone-crushing hug.

'You're a bloody idiot, Sophie Lockwood. What were you thinking?'

'I was just after more information.'

'Well next time, remain in blissful ignorance until someone is free to go exploring darkened rooms with you.' He stared into my eyes, waiting for a response. 'Promise?'

'I promise.' I hid my crossed fingers behind my back.

'Good. Now then, where's my cake?'

'I lit all the candles to make sure they worked and burnt down the kitchen.' He frowned. 'Joe's bringing it when he drops by later.'

His smile returned. 'That's more like it. I wasn't expecting to see Joe. I thought he'd be spending the evening turning the thumbscrews on Pat.'

'It'll be brief, but he reckons he can make it.'

'Well he better bloody had if he has my cake.'

'What are you moaning about now, old man?' Bill pushed his way between us and handed me a glass. 'Let the poor girl sit down.'

'So she's poor and I'm old. Exactly whose day is this?'

Mark went back to his seat and sat down, Bill giving him a playful push on the way. I lowered myself into the seat next to Craig. He offered me his glass for a toast.

'Here's to catching the bad guys.'

I took a long, cool mouthful. It was bliss.

'I said a prayer for you.'

'Thank you,' I replied. Craig knew the only times he'd catch me at a church service were Christmas, weddings and funerals, but still it was a nice thought.

'God and I both wish you'd be a bit more careful, but we also both reckon you're badass.'

I loved the idea of God sitting up on high, declaring me badass. If Craig was anything to go by, He'd also have a pint of craft beer in one hand and, after a few too many, a cigar in the other.

A ball of screwed-up wrapping paper landed in front of me. I looked up to see the culprit staring at me across the table. Joyce, wearing earrings that would have easily doubled as chandeliers and matching jewels glued on each fingernail, was eyeing me over half-moon spectacles. She discreetly gave me a little thumbs up with a questioning look.

'I'm fine,' I mouthed. She nodded, winked, and then went back to perusing the menu.

A couple of hours later, Steve and one of his team were clearing the empty plates from our table. I had devoured a large portion of fish and chips, my favourite thing on the menu. Steve's chef always manages to get the batter to a perfect level of crispiness, and the chips are chunky without doubling up as doorstops.

'Here he is, and I reckon he has dessert,' called out Mark. Joe had arrived, carrying the box that held Mark's birthday cake. He placed it carefully on the table.

'I've not got long. Catching a murderer is great, but the paper-work is a killer.' There was a collective groan around the table. 'Alright, I'm a copper, not a comedian.'

'Too right,' confirmed Bill, giving his brother a firm handshake. 'What are you drinking?'

'Coffee, please, I still have work to do.'

Bill got Steve's attention as he walked by and ordered Joe's drink.

'Come on, my sweet tooth is feeling deprived. Let's see it.' Mark reached over the table and lifted the lid. I squirmed slightly, only able to see the defects – the wobbly writing, the squished corner on one of the books, the uneven colour – but if the look on everyone else's faces was anything to go by, I was the only one who could see the mistakes.

'I love it, Sophie, it's fantastic.' Mark beamed at me.

'Well done.' Craig gave a little clap and licked his lips.

'Let's get those candles lit.' Steve, who had hovered waiting to see the cake, leant across with a cigarette lighter. I'd limited myself to ten candles – any more and I might have damaged Mark's already fragile ego. We all sang a rather painful rendition of 'Happy Birthday' that left other customers in the pub in shocked silence and, I imagine, local dogs howling.

With the cake being cut into enormous hunks by Bill, the conversation quickly turned to earlier events.

'It's a small world,' Craig commented. 'I had no idea Pat was related to Bernie.'

'None of us did,' replied Mark. 'Different surname and Pat kept very quiet about it. A few staff have been here long enough to remember Bernie, but I guess he dropped out of general consciousness. Plus the current Duke hadn't taken over running the house then; his father was still alive, so he probably didn't know much about Bernie.'

'If the Duke hadn't given me that book, we'd still have no idea of the connection and we'd all be scratching our heads and following dead ends.'

Joe sat up straight. 'No, we – the police – would be scratching our heads and… hang on a minute…' There was laughter as Joe realised what he had been about to say. 'We would be working hard and would have caught Pat before the week was out.'

'Of course you would.' I grinned and patted his shoulder as patronisingly as I could. Joe laughed and swatted my hand away.

'How's Douglas doing?' I was asking Mark, but Joe hadn't realised this and answered.

'He's a bit of a mess, to be honest, fell apart when we were questioning him. From what I've heard, he's been banging on about his publishing deal for so long now, he's worried about the damage to his reputation if he doesn't get a book out there soon.'

Mark snorted. 'Reputation? That was mainly in his head. Anyone who thought he was a great tour guide just didn't know any better, and he was never going to become a curator, not if he was doing it for the celebrity alone. People would have seen straight through him. But, if he's prepared to get stuck in and take feedback, I'll work with him and get him up to a decent standard of guiding.'

Bill put his arm around his husband's shoulders and kissed him on the cheek.

'You're a good man, Mark Boxer.'

'Hmm, you've caught me in a moment of weakness.'

Joe coughed and raised his glass.

'Anyway, this time the credit does not all belong to Ms "Sherlock" Lockwood here.' Everyone looked at Joe, wondering where he was going with this. 'The star of the show is our marvellous, glamorous, flexible Joyce Brocklehurst.'

The table erupted into roars of agreement, applause and calls for her to give a demonstration of the high kick that had saved my life. She looked momentarily bashful – not a look I ever expected to see on Joyce's face – then she quickly composed herself and told us all to:

'Keep the bloody noise down. There will be no demonstrations. To be honest, I rather surprised myself, but it turns out I haven't lost the knack. Speaking of which.'

Joyce reached into her bag, pulled out a beautifully wrapped gift with an enormous gold bow and handed it to Mark. We all watched silently as he unwrapped it.

It was a photo frame. Although none of the rest of us could see the image it contained, Mark's smile reached from ear to ear.

'But I thought you said you never joined the Tiller Girls,' he said, a little confused.

'I didn't. That was for a charity reunion about twenty years ago. Mum had already died so I dug out her old costume and went in her place.'

Mark handed the frame across to me. A slightly younger Joyce was dressed in all the finery of a Tiller Girl: a fuchsia-pink sequin-covered leotard clung to her still incredible figure. She wore fishnet stockings, a feather headdress that added over a foot to her height and matching tail feathers, and she looked magnificent.

Joyce had signed the photo to Mark and written, 'Now you can tell everyone you're friends with a Tiller Girl'. It was perfect, and a wonderful irony that on Mark's birthday, it was a woman who had made his day.

———

While Charleton House celebrates all things cycling, the cycle of life comes to an end for one of the visitors in *A Deadly Ride* .

———

The fabulous and formidable Joyce Brocklehurst has her own series of books. Be sure to join her and friend Ginger Salt as they investigate a royal murder in *Murder En Suite.*

READ THE NEXT CHARLETON HOUSE MYSTERY

If you enjoyed *Sleep Like the Dead* you'll love

A Deadly Ride.

The cycle of life and death... The joyful Cyclemania event, hosted in the breathtaking grounds of Charleton House to celebrate the Tour of Derbyshire cycle race, is drawing to a close. But the summer sun is also setting on the life of one of the visitors.

'Another charming, addictive adventure'

'Witty dialogue, outstanding characters, and a fantastic setting'

'Adams is adept at weaving mystery, mayhem, and investigation with humour'

READ A FREE CHARLETON HOUSE MYSTERY

Building a relationship with my readers is one of the best things about writing. I occasionally send newsletters with details on new releases, special offers, interviews and articles relating to The Charleton House Mysteries.

Sign up to my mailing list and you'll also receive the very first Charleton House Mystery, *A Stately Murder*.

Head to my website for your free copy and find out what happens when Sophie stumbles across the victim of the first murder Charleton House has ever known.

www.katepadams.com

ABOUT THE AUTHOR

After 25 years working in some of England's finest buildings, Kate P. Adams has turned to murder.

Kate grew up in Derbyshire, the setting for the Charleton House Mysteries, and went on to work in theatres around the country, the Natural History Museum - London, the University of Oxford and Hampton Court Palace. Every day she explored darkened corridors and rooms full of history behind doors the public never get to enter. Kate spent years in these beautiful buildings listening to fantastic tales, wondering where the bodies were hidden, and hoping that she'd run into a ghost or two.

Kate has an unhealthy obsession with finding the perfect cup of coffee, enjoys a gin and tonic, and is managed by Pumpkin, a domineering tabby cat who is a little on the large side. Now that she lives in the USA, writing the Charleton House Mysteries allows Kate to go home to be her beloved Derbyshire everyday, in her head at least.

ACKNOWLEDGEMENTS

Thank you to my wonderful beta readers Chris Bailey-Jones, Joanna Hancox, Lynne McCormack, Helen McNally, Eileen Minchin, and Rosanna Summers. Your honesty and insightful comments help make my books so much better than they would otherwise be.

Many thanks to my advance readers, your support and feedback means a great deal to me. Thank you to all my readers. I love hearing from you.

Although I worked on a number of sleepover events at Hampton Court Palace, Liz Young, Frances Sampayo and David Packer, kindly gave me their own insights.

Mark Wallis and Rosanna Summers gave me invaluable information on historical clothing.

Richard Mason, my police advisor who guides me on procedure and makes sure I am, largely, within the law. When I break the rules, that's all me!

My fabulous editor, Alison Jack, and Julia Gibbs my eagle-eyed proofreader. Both are a joy to work with.

Thank you to Susan Stark, who makes sure we have enough gin and tonic to get me though the writing process.

There is, in Scotland, a historic house called Charleton that bears no similarities to my own. Many thanks to its owner, Baron St Clair Bonde, who was happy for me to use the name. I am extremely grateful to him.

Made in the USA
Coppell, TX
16 March 2023

14314369R00111